The TREASURE HOUSE

Also by Linda Newbery

At the Firefly Gate
Lost Boy
Catcall
Nevermore
The Sandfather

The TREASURE HOUSE

Linda Newbery

Orion
Children's Books

First published in Great Britain in 2012
by Orion Children's Books
a division of the Orion Publishing Group Ltd
Orion House
5 Upper St Martin's Lane
London WC2H 9EA

An Hachette UK company

1 3 5 7 9 10 8 6 4 2

A catalogue record for this book
is available from the British Library.

Hardback ISBN 978 1 4440 0342 0
Trade paperback ISBN 978 1 4440 0343 7

Typeset by Input Data Services Ltd, Bridgwater, Somerset

Printed and bound by CPI Group (UK) Ltd, Croydon, CR0 4YY

www.orionbooks.co.uk

For Peter and Saira, with love,
and thanks for the crocodile.

Contents

Contents

1

The Elephant Bag

———◆◆◆———

If Nina had been feeling anything like her normal self, she wouldn't have sat by herself at the back of the bus. In any other mood, she'd have liked coming home across the high moorland road, instead of walking from the primary school in Chapel Street, the way she'd done for four years. Usually, she'd have loved seeing the slopes patched tawny-green in afternoon sunlight, and the stone buildings of Crowdenbridge huddled in the valley; the town looked so small, from up here, surrounded by moorland in every direction, wide and wild and windswept as far as she could see.

But today wasn't at all normal. Not a single thing about it was normal.

It wasn't just because she was wearing brand-new uniform, and starting at a big new school; she'd been ready for that, even looking forward to it. Now, though, there was only one thing she was waiting for, and that seemed no likelier to happen than it had seemed yesterday, or the day before that. Each day offered nothing but hopelessness stacked on hopelessness till it was too big a burden to carry.

For the third time since boarding the bus, Nina flicked open her mobile, just in case there was a text message. There was nothing new since Dad's **Hope u had a gd day. C u @ 5.30.**

What about Mum? What could she be doing to make her forget what *today* was? No text from her, no good luck wishes: nothing at all, not since the message Nina had saved on Sunday. She opened that one, and stared and stared, as if the words might expand themselves into new sentences that made some kind of sense.

Love you – see you soon xxx

Staring didn't help; it turned the letters into shapes and patterns that held no meaning. It was only when Nina blinked and looked out of the window that she could think at all clearly.

Soon? When was *soon*? It was Thursday now, and that message was four days old. What could have happened since, for Mum not to be in touch? Not a message, not a phone call, nothing! Nina dizzied herself every time she thought of the possibilities.

The bus was coming down into the valley now, winding its way round the steep hairpin bend that led into Church Street. It felt so different here in the town, away from the gusty moorland heights where the landscape was tinted by sun and cloud in turns. Down here it was all streets and people, traffic and busyness.

The driver stopped in the marketplace and children and teenagers piled out, their Tiptonstall uniform a stream of grey and red that broke into fragments as they went their different ways. Nina got slowly to her feet, shouldering her new rucksack, last to leave. The only people not getting off here were the handful who lived in Settlebank, on the far side of the valley.

A girl near the front looked up at Nina and smiled. 'Bye! See you tomorrow.'

'Bye,' Nina mumbled, and clumped down the steps. She was too slow to recognise, too gloomy to smile back, too late to recall that this girl was the one she'd sat next to in History.

Four girls from Nina's class at junior school had also started at Tiptonstall; most had gone to Swithinside, a much bigger school two miles in the other direction. But none of those four had been put into her form group, and she'd been too despondent to bother looking out for them at break or lunchtime. On the bus, they'd sat at the front, but Nina hadn't felt like talking. She didn't hurry to catch them up now.

This girl, the one who'd just called goodbye, had surprised Nina when she'd stood up at the end of History by being so tall that she could have been taken for a Year Nine or Ten. Nina herself was small for her age, something she'd noticed today more than ever before, as she made her way along corridors full of much bigger people. What she noticed about this

3

girl – Cat, Nina remembered, short for Caitlin – was her hair: long, fair and straight, with little plaits at the sides that looped back into her ponytail. She had an interesting pencil case, not a furry or shiny one like most people's, but made of thick purple fabric, sofa-ish, with patterned collagey bits sewn on. Perhaps she'd made it herself. Nina thought it would be stuffed with a rainbow array of gel pens, but when she glanced inside there was only one perfectly pointed pencil, a sharpener and an old-fashioned ink pen, the sort that had a nib.

Cat had been friendly, but for Nina, being friendly back felt like too much effort. Getting to the end of the day had been her only aim: a day when Dad might have heard from Mum, or found out something. He *must* have done; he *must. Perhaps*, at the very least. She would cling to *perhaps*. There couldn't be silence from Mum, and nothing but silence. It just wasn't possible. Wasn't bearable.

Nina turned the corner into Mill Street and walked along to her aunts' shop.

She loved Second-Hand Rose. There it was, between the baker's and the florist's: its door with the sign that said *Donations Welcome*, and its big front window. From habit, Nina paused before going in, because Aunt Rose's displays were always eye-catching. That was the best that could be said about them.

'There she goes, messing things about,' Aunt Nell

4

would say, tutting, but the ever-changing window, done in Aunt Rose's peculiar style, did make people stop and look. Aunt Nell had to grant that.

This week, Aunt Rose was featuring hats.

'You want to make it *seasonal*,' Aunt Nell was always telling her. 'Who's going to buy summer clothes in autumn?' But once Aunt Rose had an idea, she wouldn't be swayed. Having decided on hats, she must have put out every kind of hat she could find: flimsy summery hats, beach hats, berets and beanies, a riding helmet, a fur trapper hat with flaps that came down at the sides, and even two of those silly feathery things women wear at weddings, that made Nina think of sea anemones waving their fronds in a warm current.

Second-Hand Rose owned a rather old mannequin, known as the White Lady. She had features as pale as flour, sculpted white hair, an impossibly slender waist, long thin arms and white fingernails. Downcast as she was, Nina couldn't help giving a little smile, or at least the start of a smile. The White Lady's outfit was topped by a scarlet jester's hat with a crown of points, each tipped with a small bell. With this strange headgear, she wore a blue gingham dress, a quilted waistcoat, and silver evening gloves. As a finishing touch, Aunt Rose had belted the waistcoat by knotting an orange scarf around it.

Nina couldn't help imagining that the White Lady wore a haughty expression: part huff, part sulk. This random mishmash, she seemed to say, wasn't her style at all. She deserved better.

The doorbell jangled as Nina went in. At once Aunt Rose rushed over and crushed her in a big, perfume-scented hug.

'Sweetheart! How was your day?'

Aunt Nell was behind the till, doing something with a reel of paper. 'Hello, Nina. Come and tell us all about it.'

There were two customers in the shop: a woman on her knees, sorting through books, and an elderly man who was scowling at the shoe-rack. Nina wriggled free, because it was a bit embarrassing, the way Aunt Rose greeted her as if she'd survived a long and perilous sea-voyage. She went over to Aunt Nell, who gave her a much more restrained kiss, and a questioning glance.

For two years now, Nina had been coming to Second-Hand Rose after school, and helping her aunts – great-aunts they were, really – until Mum or Dad came to collect her on the way home from work, Dad in his van, or Mum on foot from her shift at the supermarket. Aunt Rose and Aunt Nell always wanted to hear about Nina's day – anything funny that had happened, anything silly or special, any gossip, any marvellous achievement on her part. Nina was skilled at elaborating, embroidering and even inventing; she knew how the aunts loved this part of the afternoon.

'Oh, Nina,' Aunt Rose would say. 'A ray of sunshine, you are.'

Today, though, Nina didn't feel in the least like a ray of sunshine. She felt like a creeping fog of gloom.

'It was all right, thanks,' she said. 'Fine.'

'Oh, but Nina!' Aunt Rose clasped her hands together in dismay. 'Was it really that bad?'

'She said it was fine,' said Aunt Nell, getting the till going with a little whirr.

'Oh, but I want to hear about everything! The lessons, the classrooms, the lunch, the teachers, the other children. Are they nice, Nina, the other children? Have you got a friend in your class?'

'Yes,' said Nina, because she knew that Aunt Rose wanted a *yes* so badly; 'her name's Cat. She comes home on the same bus.'

'Cat! How lovely. And does she look like a cat? Some girls do, you know, if they've got pointy cat faces and green eyes.'

'Not really. It's short for Caitlin.'

'Leave the poor girl alone!' said Aunt Nell, briskly. 'Can't you see she's tired? Nina can tell us all about it when she's ready. Why don't you leave that great muddle and make us all a nice cup of tea?'

Aunt Rose looked down at her feet. Nina saw that she'd been sorting through a big carrier bag full of oddments of wool – balls and skeins that spilled out in a multicoloured tangle.

'Yes, I think I will,' she said. 'I've made biscuits. Fat rascals, Nina, your favourites. I knew you'd be hungry.'

'Is Jake here?' Nina asked, hoping he would be.

'In the cellar, sorting,' said Aunt Nell. 'If you feel like giving him a hand, I'm sure he'd like the company.'

Nina went into the storeroom behind the shop. There was a tiny kitchen on one side, next to a flight of steps that led down to the cellar.

The cellar was big and cool, lit by dangling light bulbs. There were shelves and hangers all round the walls, and a large table in the centre. Jake, at the table, had surrounded himself with piles of books, cuddly toys, plates and dishes, pots and pans. When he heard Nina clomping down, he looked up, with his dazzling smile. It always astonished her that someone as quiet and private as Jake could have such an utterly surprising smile, as if a different, radiantly cheerful person showed himself, just for a second.

Today she was pleased to be with Jake, because he wouldn't ask questions. Jake just *was*. He was one of the volunteers who helped in the shop. Most of the others were ladies of about the aunts' age, and one or two men, but Jake was only twenty. He'd recently come out of hospital, a special hospital for people who'd had breakdowns. Nina wasn't quite sure what that meant: she imagined Jake slumped in a corner like a toy with a run-down battery, like most of the toys donated to Second-Hand Rose. Now he was getting himself going again, slowly, and Aunt Nell had told Nina that helping in the shop was a very important step for him, a sign of progress.

'You must be especially nice to him, the dear boy,' Aunt Rose said. 'Be patient. Be kind. I know you will.'

Jake was fine, as long as he didn't have to speak to customers. He preferred to be down in the cellar, sorting, humming along to tunes on the radio. Nina liked sorting, too, so they often spent an hour or two together in the afternoons, not saying much, just the occasional 'What on earth d'you think *this* is?' or 'I can't imagine anyone wearing *that*, can you?' as they fished various items out of the bags.

What Nina liked about going through the donations was that you never knew what might turn up. Among the scrumpled clothes and the chipped teapots there might be something really valuable – a diamond necklace, perhaps, or a small carved ornament that turned out to be a priceless work of art from Japan. Neither of these things actually *had* turned up, but it was fun to imagine. Her job and Jake's was to sort stuff into categories – belts, children's clothes, toys – for the aunts to look at later. Any hopelessly worn or shabby clothes would go for fabric recycling; others were washed and ironed and put out on the display racks. Items that might be valuable were put aside for Aunt Nell, who knew quite a lot, and had an antiques-dealer friend who would look at anything she thought promising. Nina had been disappointed several times, though, by finding what she thought were diamonds or gold, only to have them dismissed by Aunt Nell as worthless and put in the fifty pence tray.

'*Ooo - werrr – ta-da-da-da – oooo,*' sang Jake, with the radio.

Nina dumped her rucksack on the floor. 'What shall I start on?'

'Bags there,' Jake said, nodding towards the corner, where Nina saw the usual collection of bursting and overflowing sacks, bags and boxes. She cuddled the biggest black sack and lifted it, her face turned against the plasticky softness. Her sideways glance lighted on the shelf where handbags and holdalls were stacked, and smaller bags hung from hooks. Something jumped out at her with startling familiarity. She laid the bin-bag on the table, and turned back, staring, then went closer, to touch.

A fabric bag, indigo-blue, with a large appliqué elephant in shades of turquoise, embroidered with silver threads.

Mum's elephant bag. Her favourite. A bag that Mum would never give away, ever. Not even to Second-Hand Rose.

2

The Green Crocodile

————◆————

'What's *that* doing here?' Nina demanded.

Jake stood rigid with panic for a moment, then turned slowly and focused. Whenever anyone asked him a direct question, he thought he'd been caught doing something wrong.

Nina hadn't meant to shout. 'It's my mum's bag, you see,' she told him, lowering the volume several notches. 'And Mum's disappeared. Gone. No one knows where.' It was no good; her voice trembled. She couldn't say those things in a matter-of-fact way.

'Oh. Yes,' said Jake, as if he knew already. The aunts must have told him. They'd probably said, 'Be nice to Nina,' just as Aunt Rose had told Nina to be nice to Jake.

'How long has it been here?' Nina asked, fizzing with frustration, because Jake just couldn't be hurried. She picked up the bag, smelled it, unfastened the loop at the top that held it together and looked inside for some clue or message. But it held none of Mum's familiar clutter:

lip-salves, perfume spray, spare socks or a cardigan. It was completely empty.

Jake put on his concentrating face, an expression that made his gaze seem to disappear inside his head. 'Someone brought it in,' he said, after several moments' thought.

'But how could that have happened? It's my mum's bag! She uses it when she goes to yoga – she'd never give it away!'

'Dunno. Saw it here … um … Tuesday.'

'Tuesday? How could it have been Tuesday?'

Jake just looked back at her, not understanding the weirdness of Mum's bag being here in the cellar when no one had seen anything of Mum herself since last Friday.

'Tuesday. Definitely,' he told her. 'P'raps it's not hers. Another one the same. Where'd she get it?'

'I don't know. She's had it ages.'

'Might be lots of them,' said Jake.

'No, this is Mum's. I know it's hers.' Nina bent over the bag, and pushed her face inside. There was the faintest smell of Mum's perfume, sweet and spicy. Patchouli, it was called. Other elephant bags might exist, but it was too much to believe that there was another one in Crowdenbridge, identical to Mum's and smelling of the same perfume she wore.

'Tea's ready, darlings!' called Aunt Rose from the top of the steps. 'Shall I bring it down, or are you coming up?'

The aunts would know how and when the bag had got here. Spending most of his time in the cellar, Jake didn't usually see the donations until he started unpacking them.

'We'll come up,' Nina shouted back. 'OK, Jake?'

She saw the look of doubt cross his face; then he swallowed and made himself taller. 'Yeah.'

Still holding the elephant bag, Nina went first up the stairs. Jake kept close behind, as if he might lose his nerve and bolt back down unless he did it quickly, in one go. They reached the top with a sense of triumph. Nina glanced through to the shop to see if it was suddenly thronging with customers, but there was only one, the man who came in every week to look for railway books.

'Here we are, loves.' Aunt Rose came out of the kitchen with a tray, and looked round for somewhere to put it down. 'Jake, sweetheart, can you move that crocodile?'

A green velvet crocodile, nearly as long as the spread of Nina's arms, sat on top of the chest of drawers. It had a ferocious expression and big pointy teeth that gaped wide, revealing a blood-red lining to its mouth.

Jake picked it up and looked at it, puzzled. 'Been here before.'

'Has it?' Nina wasn't much interested.

'Yeah. I sorted it last week. Someone bought it, same day.' Jake upended the crocodile in an umbrella-stand, where only its bright green tail stuck out. Nina couldn't help thinking how uncomfortable that looked, so put it the other way up, with its double row of teeth snarling at the ceiling.

'Here's the fat rascals. I know you both like them,' said Aunt Rose. On a plate were two big round biscuits, with faces: glacé-cherry eyes, and grimacing almond teeth that were almost as fierce as the crocodile's. 'Help yourselves.'

Nina loved fat rascals, but she hardly glanced at them. 'Aunt Rose, when did this come in?' She held up the bag. 'It's my mum's – but she didn't bring it, did she? She couldn't have.'

'No, dear. Your dad brought a couple of boxes in, though.'

'*Dad* did?'

'Yes. Now, when would that have been?' Aunt Rose frowned deeply. 'Yes. Yes. Last Wednesday it must have been, or was it Thursday? Said your mum was having a clear-out.'

Nina tried the phrase in her head. A clear-out? People talked about *clearing out* stuff, but they also said *clear out* the way you might say *clear off.* But Dad couldn't have meant that. He hadn't known, then.

'Yes, that's what he said,' Aunt Rose went on, nodding. 'Brought in two or three cardboard boxes. Clothes, mostly.'

'Jake said Tuesday, didn't you, Jake?' said Nina.

Jake nodded. 'Um. *This* Tuesday.'

14

'Mm, that would be right,' said Aunt Rose. 'We were so chock-full last week, I put a lot of stuff in the shed out the back. It wasn't till Monday that Ivy brought it all in. I think it was Ivy – Monday's the day she usually comes. Nell was out, and we were busy with customers, so Ivy didn't have time for much sorting. She probably took the bag downstairs just before we closed, so Jake didn't see it till Tuesday. That makes sense.' Absent-mindedly, she broke a piece off the remaining fat rascal and put it in her mouth, then realised and handed the rest to Nina. 'Eat this, dear, while there's still some left.'

'So Mum had a big sort-out just before she went.' Nina felt certain that this was a Clue. 'What else was in the boxes? Can you remember?'

'No, dear, I'm afraid I don't know. You can ask Ivy, but she won't be in again till next week.'

'Jake? Can you remember what else was there?'

Jake shook his head slowly. 'Loads of stuff from the shed. Don't remember anything special.'

Oh, this was so *frustrating*! Nina gazed around the storeroom, at the clothes hanging on rails waiting for Aunt Nell to price them and put them out in the shop. Were some of Mum's clothes here? Why? Which clothes had she thrown out, and which had she taken with her, wherever she'd gone?

What could have made Mum behave in such a baffling, utterly un-Mum-like way? Nina just couldn't understand it.

15

Last Friday. Such a bright, end-of-holidayish afternoon it had seemed, the sun shining in a leisurely sort of way, time passing with no sense of hurry. Nina had gone out with her friend Max, his parents and Zebedee the dog for a picnic by Crowdenwater. They'd hired a boat, taking it in turns to row, and had landed on a tiny island in the middle of the lake, pretending to be shipwrecked.

The only sadness hanging over the day was that Max and Nina wouldn't go to school together any more, because Max was starting at Sir Frank Dalloway, an all-boys' school in Hattersfield. He'd be catching the train every morning, not the bus like Nina. They'd been friends ever since starting at Crowdenbridge Juniors, and Nina would miss him. They'd still be friends, but it wouldn't be the *same*.

Soon after six, Max's parents had dropped Nina off at home. She waved goodbye and went indoors, a little sun-dazed, arms tired from rowing. She was looking forward to telling her parents about the picnic and the island, and how Zebedee had loved swimming, and had showered everyone with water when he shook himself dry.

'Mum? Dad?' she shouted, inside the front door.

If Mum was in, she'd usually call back from somewhere in the house, and come hurrying. Nina remembered that it was Friday, Mum's late shift at the

Co-op, so she wouldn't be home yet. But when Dad appeared, something about the slowness of his walk and the set of his shoulders told her that something was wrong.

He tried to smile. 'Had a good time?'

'Brilliant, thanks. What's up?'

'It's ... well ...' Dad shook his head. 'I'm not ...'

'What? What is it?'

'Mum's not here. She ... she ... I just came in and ...'

It wasn't unusual for Mum to be out, of course, but what *was* unusual was Dad's inability to finish a sentence.

'It's a late Co-op day,' Nina reminded him.

'No, I don't mean that. I mean she's ... well, gone.'

'Gone? Gone where?'

'I don't really ... don't really know ...'

Nina was looking past him, through the door into the kitchen; she swivelled her gaze up the stairs for a glimpse of Mum. 'What? Has something happened? Is she in hospital?'

'No, no.' Dad put an arm round her shoulders and guided her to the sitting-room sofa. He swallowed, and tried again. 'I don't understand it, Nina. She's ... she's gone. Just gone. Left a note on the kitchen table.' He got up and fetched it.

Nina read, *Gone away for a while. Please don't worry. Love you both very much. Miranda x x x x x x x x x x*

It was written in purple ink, on a page torn off the pad Mum and Dad used for shopping lists. The paper

17

had narrow lines on it, but Mum's swoopy, loopy handwriting was much too large to fit between them, so she'd turned the page sideways.

The writing blurred in front of Nina's eyes. She made herself focus, and read it a second and a third time.

'What does she mean? *Gone away for a while?* What sort of while?'

'I don't know, love. I've tried her mobile, but it's not turned on.'

'*Please don't worry?* What? How can she expect us not to worry, if she disappears without saying *where*?'

'I don't know, love, I really don't.'

'Has she gone to one of her friends? Does Tiffany know? Mum was there this morning.'

'I haven't rung anyone yet. I'll try Tiffany now.'

Dad fetched Mum's address book from the kitchen shelf, and Nina waited in a haze of bewilderment while he keyed in the number. Tiffany ran the dance and yoga studio where Mum taught classes on Tuesday and Friday mornings; if Mum had gone away, Tiffany would surely know. Maybe she'd know for how *long*.

'Hello, Tiffany, it's Richard Bickerstaff, Miranda's— No, she's not here. I thought you might ... oh. Oh! Sorry ... no, no, I don't.'

There was a lot of listening, and more *oh*-ing, and bottom-lip biting, before Dad thanked Tiffany and said he'd let her know if he heard anything. He turned to Nina in puzzlement.

'Apparently Mum went in today, taught her yoga group as usual, then told Tiffany she'd have to find someone else to take the classes for a while. Tiffany's not very pleased about it, being left in the lurch at short notice. She's trying to find someone to cover.'

'Are you sure Mum's not at the Co-op? That's where she'd usually be.'

Dad made another phone call, and finished it looking even more baffled. 'She hasn't been there today. Left a message, early, to say she couldn't go in. No reason.'

'But – early – I was *here*! Why wouldn't she *tell* us if she had to go somewhere?'

'I don't know, precious. I don't know what's going on.'

They sat down, Dad cuddling Nina, both gazing at the note as if more words, in invisible ink, might choose to reveal themselves if stared at hard enough. Nina's mind raced with possible and impossible explanations, while Dad tried to make the situation sound normal. 'She'll be back, you'll see. Gone to visit a friend, I expect.'

'But why would—'

'Took it into her head and off she went. You know what Mum's like.'

'But then why didn't she ...' The unfinished-sentence thing seemed to be infectious.

Dad shook his head, then nodded. 'She'll phone later, I bet. Had a train to catch and left in a hurry.'

'A train to *where*, though?' Nina felt dizzy with all the places trains could go, linking up with other trains, or with boats, or planes. If someone wanted to get away, there was the whole *world.*

'I'm just guessing.'

Nina stood up. 'Dad, don't you think we should, you know, phone the ...'

He looked at her. 'Phone the police, you're thinking? But what would I tell them? A grown woman's decided to go away for a while, leaving us a note? No. We'll have to wait and see.'

But the frightening thing for Nina was that Dad didn't know any more than she did. She knew he was only pretending not to be worried, for her sake.

3

The Fringed Scarf

———•─•───

It had been so horrible, that Friday evening, that Nina kept going over and over it until her brain refused to do any more proper remembering. Everything she and Dad had said was stored in there, but it might as well have been a play, acted by strangers. She couldn't help thinking it was a bad dream, and that she'd go home and find Mum getting supper, cooking in her own special way, adding a sprinkle of this or a dash of that, getting side-tracked writing notes for herself or reading the local paper, but always serving up something delicious, even if not entirely recognisable. Dad wasn't much of a cook at all. Since Mum had gone, he and Nina had been eating sausages with lettuce, most nights. But that was the least of Nina's problems.

Even now, she couldn't help half expecting Mum to be there at home when she got in: busy, distracted in several directions at once, but remembering to ask about the first day at Tiptonstall.

'Are they all right, dears?' said Aunt Rose, meaning the fat rascals.

'Oh, yes – better than all right.' Nina hadn't finished hers yet and suddenly felt wearied and full, but Aunt Rose looked so eager that she attempted a smile and took one more bite.

Nina considered the new information that Mum had had a sort-out, just before she left. *What* had she sorted, and why? What had she brought into the shop, and what might it reveal about where she was planning to go? There must be things of Mum's still here.

'Jake,' she said, 'do you mind if I—'

At that moment the door of the changing room opened and someone stepped out. It wasn't much of a changing room, just a cupboard with a light bulb and a mirror and one hook, but it had to do. Nina hadn't realised anyone was in there, and neither, obviously, had Jake; at once he sidled towards the back of the storeroom, behind the hanging-rail. Nina looked at the girl who'd come out. She was tall and thin, with rust-coloured hair piled up messily. Turning, she looked at herself in the mirror, swaying one way and then the other. She wore a short black jacket with embroidery on the sleeves, a flared red skirt, and a fringed scarf tied round her hips.

Nina let out a yip – not because the outfit looked brilliant, which it did, but because that scarf was one of Mum's.

In her hand the girl held a black trilby hat. She unfastened the clip that held up her hair, releasing waves and kinks that tumbled down her back. Then she put on the hat, the finishing touch, and tilted it to one side.

Aunt Rose beamed, and clapped her hands. 'Oh, wonderful! *Très chic!* Do come and look, Nell, dear!'

Nina was quite *sure* the scarf was Mum's, even though she hadn't seen it for some while. It was burgundy coloured, fringed, with a pattern of turquoise birds. Nina remembered Mum wearing it round her shoulders, and once she'd lent it to Nina to throw over her head when it was raining.

Nina got up from the floor, where she'd been sitting cross-legged to eat her fat rascal. 'Did you find all those things here?'

The girl turned round. 'Yes, isn't it great? There's always something interesting.' She had a striking face – not in the least bit pretty, but unexpectedly beautiful, with a long, bony nose, a wide mouth, and calm eyes under the rim of the hat. And the springy fox-red hair, so vibrant that it seemed to have a life of its own.

At once Nina wanted to *be* her.

The girl smiled at Nina, looked curiously at Jake's feet – all that could be seen of him behind the hanging-rail dense with clothes – and went back into the cupboard.

'Are you going to buy all of it?' Nina asked the closed door.

'I'll have to count up my money,' the girl's voice answered.

You can't have that scarf, Nina wanted to say, but how could she stop this girl, or anyone else, from buying something that was for sale? It didn't belong to Mum any more, and it was hardly likely that she'd sewn secret messages into the hem, expecting Nina to find them. And wouldn't Mum be pleased for her scarf to go to someone who'd wear it so stylishly?

She was thinking the way she might if Mum were *dead*!

Stop it. *Stop* it.

She'd better get used to this. There might be people in the street wearing clothes of Mum's, and there was nothing wrong with that, since Mum had donated them.

What she could hardly bear was the thought of another night of waiting. Another Mum-less evening at home, with nothing happening. Many more like that, and it would start to seem normal.

❦

At five o'clock, Aunt Nell turned the OPEN sign on the door to CLOSED. Jake left, and the aunts spent the next half-hour cashing up and tidying. Nina went down to the cellar for her rucksack; when she returned, Dad was standing by the till with Aunt Nell.

'Don't you worry about Nina,' Aunt Nell was saying.
'And here she is,' Dad said brightly, pulling Nina to

him for a hug and a kiss. 'Nina, I thought we'd go out to eat, just the two of us. You must be sick of burnt sausages. And you can tell me all about your day.'

He had a faint sprinkling of sawdust in his eyebrows, as he often did. His work, just now, was at one of the farms on the Settlebank side of the valley, where he was making new banisters for the farmhouse stairs.

'Dad, I've got something to show you first. Come with me.' Nina ran ahead of him down the cellar steps, and took the elephant bag down from the shelf where she'd tucked it out of sight, not wanting anyone to buy it. 'Mum's special bag! And there must be other things of hers here, too, like that old scarf with birds on it. Someone's just bought that. But *this* – Mum's yoga bag – what's it doing here?'

Dad looked just as startled as Nina had been. He reached out and touched the elephant's trunk.

'You didn't know? But Aunt Rose said you brought it!' Nina told him. 'With some other stuff of Mum's.'

'Did I? No. Surely not. I did drop off three cardboard boxes – Mum asked me to. But—'

'She wouldn't give this away!'

'No, she wouldn't.' Dad picked up the bag and turned it in his hands. 'P'raps it's another one just like Mum's.'

'It's not! There can't be two the same. And it smells of Mum.'

Dad held the handles to his ears and pushed his face inside, like a horse with a nosebag. 'Yes, it does,' he

25

agreed rather sadly, coming out. 'It does seem odd, but Mum must have decided to part with it when she had her clear-out. It would have been in one of the boxes. I didn't look inside, just carted them all to the van.'

'Didn't Mum say *why* she was having a clear-out? Was she, you know, planning to—'

'As far as I know, it was because I'd put up those new shelves in our bedroom cupboard. I took everything out, to do the work, and she decided it was time for a sort-through. We'd been shoving things into that cupboard for years.'

'But the elephant bag wouldn't have been buried in there.'

'No, it wouldn't,' said Dad. 'I'm as surprised as you are to see it here.'

'Richard?' Aunt Nell shouted down the stairs. 'Are you ready? We're about to lock up.'

'Coming!' Dad called back, then said to Nina, 'Do you want it, the bag? I'll buy it for you.'

Upstairs, Aunt Nell said that the till was locked, and that anyway they needn't pay for the bag, since it seemed to have been brought in by mistake.

'Bye, then, darling. You have a lovely meal with your dad.' Aunt Rose was looking pink and excited for some reason. 'We'll see you ... soon.'

Dad and Nina went to Pumpernickel, Mum's favourite vegetarian café. Nina had never had a meal there, but a few times Mum had brought her in for juice and a cranberry muffin, or to buy food to eat at home. As they sat at a corner table and studied the menu, Dad was trying to sound cheerful. Nina wished he wouldn't; cheerful didn't feel right at all. And the items chalked on the blackboard only made her remember that falafels were Mum's favourite, and that hummus was one of the things they often had at home.

'So – not too bad, then?' Dad said, when Nina had given minimal details of her day at school.

She shrugged. 'Suppose not. You still haven't heard anything, have you? You'd have said.'

'No. Sorry. Not a peep. But, Nina …'

His apologetic tone made her look at him suspiciously.

'The thing is,' he said, 'I need to go and look for Mum. Go away for a few days.'

'But – how? Look where?'

Dad sighed. 'I can't stay at home and do nothing. Can't wait around for her to turn up.'

'So you know where she is, then?' Nina accused.

'No. No, I don't. But there's a few places I could try.'

'But what about work? Your customers? That staircase you're doing?'

'That's the good thing about being my own boss. It's not a great time to go away, but I can put people off till I get back, then work like mad to catch up. And Nina, precious, I promise to phone every night and tell you where I am, and send you lots of texts as well. I'm not going to disappear, like—' He stopped himself, and tried again. 'I'm really not going to disappear.'

'But *I* want to come, too!'

'No, precious, you know that's impossible. Not when you've just started at big school – it's no time to go away. Things are disrupted enough as it is. I've been talking to the aunts, and they're happy for you to stay with them while I'm not here. They're delighted, actually – they'll love having you. So what we'll do, when we've finished eating, is go home for some of your things, and then I'll take you round.'

'To*night*?'

'I want to make an early start. Now that I've made up my mind, there's no point hanging around. OK, love?' He took hold of her arm, and waggled it. 'I knew you'd be a good, sensible girl. Now, what shall we have to eat?'

4

The China Seahorse

—◆●◆—

'Are you ready yet?' Dad called up the stairs.

Nina had to tiptoe back to her own room before replying. 'Nearly!'

She didn't want Dad to know that she'd been gazing into Mum's half of the double wardrobe, rather than sorting out her own things. What had Mum been thinking, last time she stood there? What had she packed? Surely she must have packed *something*, though Nina couldn't immediately see what was missing. With more time, she could go through Mum's clothes and try to work out what wasn't there. That must give some kind of clue. Wouldn't the police want to know that sort of detail, if—

No. This wasn't a police matter. Dad had said so. Mum had gone away because she wanted to, for some reason Nina couldn't begin to fathom. It wasn't because anyone had *made* her. What could she have been thinking? It wasn't right. It wasn't *fair*.

In Nina's hand was a small Buddha, carved in polished

green stone. She'd picked it up from Mum's bedside table, wanting something of Mum's to take with her, as a kind of good-luck charm. The Buddha was sitting in lotus position (Mum could do that, though Nina's legs simply refused to bend themselves so far) and had an expression of such calmness and wisdom that Nina almost thought he might tell her something.

He didn't, and she had her own packing to do. She slid him into the side pocket of the sports bag Dad had lent her.

Toothbrush, hairbrush, knickers, jeans, tops, clean shirts for school, a couple of books – she slung them all in. She wished she didn't have to do this. It didn't feel right that the house would soon be empty, that no one would be here to welcome Mum, if – no, *when* – she came home.

❧

It wasn't that Nina didn't like staying with her great-aunts. She did. They were the nearest thing she had to grandmothers, because Mum had no family apart from Dad and Nina, and Dad's mother had died when he was very young, so he'd been brought up by Aunt Rose and Aunt Nell, who were his mother's sisters, and their husbands, Uncles Eric and Derek. Nina knew Uncle Eric only from photographs, as he'd died when she was just a year old.

The two aunts and Uncle Derek lived two streets

away from the shop. Nina liked the oddness of their tall old house: it was set on the steep street that climbed the hill, and the front door was much lower than the back, with only the entrance and kitchen on the ground floor. All the other rooms were upstairs, and to get to the garden you went up to the first-floor sitting room and then out through French windows. The garden was a small one, with high walls and hardly any grass, but from one corner, where the aunts had put a bench and a table for eating outside, you could look down into the tops of the almond trees on the pavement. The aunts' bedrooms were up another flight of stairs, and Nina's room was on its own in the attic, with sloping eaves that meant she had to be careful not to bang her head.

It was when Uncle Eric died, leaving an unexpectedly large sum of money, that Aunt Rose had decided to fulfil her dream of running a shop for charity. Till then, she'd worked in the Post Office, but she was very absent-minded and not reliable with paperwork — always putting forms and letters in the wrong places, and hardly ever getting the money to add up. Aunt Nell would have been good at Post Office work, but she had a job in the knitting shop, where she was frustrated by the lack of business opportunities, and thoroughly bored with discussions about buttonholes, cable-stitch and possible shrinkage.

When Aunt Rose saw a vacant shop in Mill Street, with a big front window, she took her chance. She had

Matthew and Son, Ironmongers painted out, and *Second-Hand Rose* painted in, in flamboyant purple letters decorated with pink roses.

'I never thought she'd make it work,' Aunt Nell had told Nina, 'and you should have seen the muddle she got into at first. Can't say no to anyone, Rose can't, not to save her life.'

So the shop, for the first year or two, had been crammed full of useless donations – big bulky things that no one would ever buy, like mildewed sets of encyclopaedia, old-fashioned prams with wonky wheels, and weighty sewing-machines. Eventually Aunt Rose would have to pay the council to take them away. She was trying to do everything herself, with no helpers. The shop was so cluttered that customers could hardly get inside; when they did, their feet skidded on discarded bin-bags or got tangled in trailing wires. Aunt Rose was making no money at all, and it looked as if she'd have to give up her dream. Then Aunt Nell had stepped in. Well, someone had to; that was her view. 'That sister of mine hasn't got a grain of business sense. Left to herself, she'd have ended up trapped in the cellar, buried under a mountain of rubbish.'

But, as Aunt Rose saw it, *nothing* should be dismissed as rubbish. That was the point. 'Everything has a use. It's a matter of imaginative recycling, and the right person coming along.'

Together they made a good partnership: Aunt

Nell's common sense, grasp of accounting, and knack of organising the volunteers, alongside Aunt Rose's imagination, and her love of people and their stories. Aunt Rose really didn't mind that there were people who came in just to chat, like Mr Ellis who had only ever bought one tarnished silver egg-cup, or Mrs Freeman who loved to relate every detail of her many illnesses, for the price of a paperback book; or the woman who dropped in every week to look through the children's clothes and complain that everything was too expensive.

Aunt Nell had snorted like a sneezing horse, the first time she heard that. 'Expensive! Compared to what? Does she think we're here to *give* things away?'

Aunt Rose really *would* give things away if she could make someone happy by doing so, but under Aunt Nell's stern eye the shop started to bring in money. All the profits, once the expenses had been covered, went to the local hospital. The aunts didn't make anything for themselves, but had enough to live on with their pensions and some interest from their savings.

'Well, it keeps us out of mischief!' Aunt Rose said. 'Gives us something to do.'

But Second-Hand Rose was more than that. It was their lives. Nina couldn't possibly imagine the aunts without Second-Hand Rose, or Second-Hand Rose without the aunts. They belonged together.

The guest bedroom was a frilly, quilty, gauzy sort of place. Nina didn't usually like frills or gauze, but this room made her feel like a girl in a story, as if she might part the curtains and gaze out at misty mountains and distant turrets. What she actually did see was Market Street, a line of parked cars and the craft gallery opposite, but when she lay in bed – under a sort of billowing canopy that draped itself around the pillows – she couldn't help having story-heroine thoughts.

The aunts always made her feel special, too. Right now, even though Nina was still full of delicious Pumpernickel food, Aunt Rose was down in the kitchen making hot chocolate, a bedtime drink. It was quite rare for Nina to sleep at the aunts' house, as home was only four streets away in Royds Row, but a few times she'd stayed when Mum and Dad were going out for the evening. Mum had said that having Nina to stay was a big treat for Aunt Rose and Aunt Nell. 'You must remember that, sweetheart, and appreciate the effort they go to.'

Mum *used* to say, Nina thought miserably, as she unpacked her things. When would Mum be around again, with all the Mum-sayings Nina found herself missing?

The coat-hangers in the wardrobe were quilted in satiny fabric, with ribbon-ties around the hooks. Nina put her school uniform away, and the few other clothes she'd brought with her, and sat on the bed.

This was just weird: the suddenness of Dad's decision, the speed of her arrival here. In spite of everything Dad had said, Nina couldn't see how his plan would work. If he really knew nothing about where Mum had gone, how could he start looking? *Where?* But he'd been insistent that he had to try. What would he do? Drive up and down motorways, walk round streets, hoping for a glimpse of Mum?

'You will come back, won't you?' Nina had asked him, several times, and he'd assured her that of course he would.

'I'll be gone for about a week. Two weeks, maybe. Unless I find Mum sooner, of course.'

But two weeks seemed an immensely long time, and what if it stretched into three or four? What if Dad *didn't* come back, however much he meant to? What if first Mum and then Dad got sucked into some alternative dimension, some other world?

No, that's just silly, Nina told herself. Time to get ready for bed. She picked up her wash-bag and went down to the bathroom on the floor below.

The bathroom was all pink and white, smelling of lavender and lily of the valley, with a ruched blind, tufted bath mat and a whole array of wrapped soaps and bath salts in stoppered bottles. It was so feminine a room that Nina couldn't imagine Uncle Derek clomping about in here, or shaving in front of the mirror.

As she went to the sink, a china seahorse in silvery

grey looked at her from the window sill.

She stared at it, at its bobble eyes, fine fluted nose and spiny spine, and the curl of tail that swept down to the flat stand it balanced on.

She'd last seen that seahorse on Mum's dressing table.

❦

'Oh, dear,' said Aunt Rose, coming up the kitchen stairs and meeting Nina on the way down. 'I didn't realise. I saw it in the shop a couple of days ago and thought it would go nicely in the bathroom, so I bought it. I've always liked seahorses. So it was your mum's? Ivy must have put it out.'

She was carrying a big mug of chocolate, which she set down on the halfway window ledge so that she could give Nina a hug.

'*Is* my mum's,' Nina said, though her face was squashed against Aunt Rose's arm. '*Is.*'

'Yes, of course. Is. Poor dear! That must have given you a surprise.'

'What's going on?' said Aunt Nell, coming out of the sitting room.

Nina explained, adding, 'It's not Mum giving stuff to the shop that's so weird. The point is, she's given some of her *favourite* things. This seahorse lives on her dressing table, with her make-up and stuff. And there's the elephant bag. Why would she get rid of them?'

The aunts tried to gloss over it. 'We all get fed up with

the same old things,' Aunt Nell said, and Aunt Rose added, 'I expect she just fancied a change.'

Aunt Nell gave her sister a reproachful glare, while the remark dropped into the stairwell, heavy with meaning. Nina picked it up.

'Fancied a change? What, like change *everything* – change her whole life?'

'No, no, that's not what I mean,' said Aunt Rose, in a fluster. 'I didn't mean – I was only talking about *things*.'

❦

When she'd finished the hot chocolate, Nina remembered the jade Buddha. She delved into the side pocket of the sports bag, brought out the green stone figure and placed it on the bedside table.

'Bring Mum back,' she pleaded, and touched the Buddha's head; then got into bed and turned out the lamp.

As soon as she closed her eyes, the seahorse, the fringed scarf, the elephant bag and the Buddha began to whirl round in her mind, in a taunting dance.

It wasn't Mum who'd taken the stuff to Second-Hand Rose, was it? It was *Dad*. What if he'd decided to throw out some of Mum's things? Did that make any sense at all? It had been on Wednesday or Thursday when he'd brought the boxes in, and Mum had left on Friday. Could Mum have flown into a temper when she found her things missing, and flounced out of the house?

But she hadn't flounced. She'd walked calmly along the street with Nina, and had told Tiffany about not being able to take the yoga classes. Dad genuinely didn't know what had made her walk out. And surely she wouldn't leave Dad – leave *Nina* – in such a mysterious way, just because of a few belongings.

Nina couldn't fathom it out. She sat up in bed, reached for her mobile phone – which she always left on, always near her, just in case – and texted a message.

Mum? Where are you? Why can't you txt?

She'd hardly put the phone down before it gave the little trickle of notes that meant a message was arriving. Her hands were shaking as she read it.

I'm OK. Hope you are too. Don't worry. Love you lots. Mum xxx

At once Nina tried calling, but – maddeningly – got only voicemail. Why couldn't Mum leave her phone *on*?

'Mum, where are you?' she said to the messaging service. 'Can't you ring me? Just ring me?'

She lay down, her face turned sideways so that she could fix her eyes on the mobile. But, no matter how hard she stared, it remained silent.

5

The Indigo Rosette

———◦◆◦———

In the morning, Nina woke to the realisation that it was
a week since she'd seen Mum – a whole week since
they'd parted last Friday morning, outside Tiffany's
studio. Many times, Nina had gone over the final
moments to see if she could find overlooked significance
in anything Mum had said or done. She remembered
waiting by the front door while Mum rushed back
upstairs for something she'd forgotten, but that wasn't
at all unusual. That had made her a bit late, so she and
Nina had marched briskly through the market square
and into Lower Street. What had they talked about?
Nina couldn't even remember; quite likely they hadn't
said much at all, as they'd been walking so fast.

'Bye then, darling. Have a lovely time with Max.'
Nina remembered that, and Mum kissing the top of
her head. Then Mum went inside. There had been
no protracted farewell, no wistful gazing. And Nina
couldn't remember looking back at Mum either, in her
hurry to get to Max's.

Surely there must be *something* – something a bit different, or suspicious? Mum had known by then that she was going – because, as Nina now knew, she'd already made the phone call to the Co-op. Surely there must have been a hint of sadness or regret in that last goodbye? But as soon as Nina thought she remembered, a doubt crept in; maybe she was making it up, because she didn't want to believe that Mum could leave her and Dad without the most enormous wrench.

It was nicer, if sadder, to think of Mum as she usually was. Mum practising yoga in her bedroom, with the Indian music she liked as accompaniment, twisting and stretching herself into impossible-looking poses and balances. Mum spending a whole Saturday cooking, throwing herself into it, making pastry and sauces and mousses, using – as Dad complained – every available spoon, bowl and dish, till the sink was piled high with washing-up. Mum in the sitting room, completely absorbed in a book, reading until the light went dim but not stirring from her chair to turn on the lamp. Mum helping with schoolwork – she was good at English, excellent at French, which Nina had started in Year Six, but not much use at all with Maths. It always had to be Dad who helped with Maths.

Mum was Mum – interested in so many things, full of energy, always cheerful, always busy. She was always around, scattering her belongings through the house in a colourful trail, making plans, suggesting nice things to do at the weekend.

Always *had* been around.

Now something had happened to make Mum think that somewhere else was more important than home. Something or someone was more important than Nina and Dad. A letter, a phone call, an unexpected visitor?

But why wouldn't Mum have *said*?

Round and round and round went Nina's thoughts, knotting and tangling themselves, getting nowhere she hadn't been before, till she felt like shouting out loud to drive them away. The frustration and worry had solidified inside her as a dull ache in her stomach, sometimes sharpening into actual pain.

There *must* be an answer. But where should she start looking?

※

'Caitlin Eagleton?'

'Here, sir.'

'Harry Farnes?'

'Here, sir.'

'Georgina Fleming?'

'Here, sir.'

'Nina Flyte-Bickerstaff?'

Oh, no – not again. There were titters from the back row. Nina's face went hot, and she answered in a mumble.

The Geography teacher, Mr Aldbourne, looked up

short-sightedly. 'Nina Flyte-Bickerstaff, put your hand up, please.'

Reluctantly Nina did so. The teacher said, 'Well, Nina. Everyone else so far has managed to answer politely. Do you think perhaps you could do the same? Shall we try again?'

Oh, no. Please let's not.

'Nina Flyte-Bickerstaff?' Mr Aldbourne repeated.

'Here, sir,' Nina said clearly. 'Only it's Bickerstaff. Just Bickerstaff. I should be in the Bs.' She'd known what was coming when he'd passed smoothly through Baker, Barford, Bavishi and Blake.

'Oh! Sorry – I'll change it.' Mr Aldbourne made a note. He seemed quite nice really, as far as she could tell after five minutes: youngish, and even a bit nervous himself. Someone had said that he was new too. But he'd just given Nina an embarrassment she'd rather not have had. The two girls behind her, Jem and Tash, thought 'Flyte-Bickerstaff' was hilarious. Yesterday, after hearing it for the first time, they'd come up behind Nina in the corridor to taunt her with, 'Ooh, look, it's her ladyship Flyte-Bickerstaff!' in upper-class voices, and, 'Did you forget your tiara? How will you manage without your maid? Must be awful, away from your stately home – having to mix with plebs like us!'

Nina rounded on them. 'It's not like that! I'm not posh. Or rich. It's just my mum's name and my dad's, that's all.'

But they'd giggled all the more, and skipped off, still exchanging snooty nonsense. Now they'd do it all over again.

At the first chance, at break-time, Nina went to the office and told the secretary there that her name was Bickerstaff. The secretary, who wore a great deal of powdery make-up and a necklace made of green tiddlywinks, looked at her computer screen.

'Oh! I've got Flyte-Bickerstaff here. If you want it changed you'll need to get your mum or dad to phone in and confirm it.'

'I can't. They're not here.'

'No, but you can get them to phone tomorrow.'

'No.' Nina tried again. 'I mean they're both *away*. At the moment.'

'Oh.' The secretary gave her a puzzled look. 'So who's looking after you, then?'

'My aunts. I'm staying with them.'

'I'd better take down details. Can you give me their address and phone number, just in case we need to get in touch while your parents are away?'

Nina gave her aunts' address and number, wishing she hadn't bothered trying. It sounded like a change of address. It sounded *permanent*. In any case, was it really a good idea to jettison Mum's part of her name? Was it admitting the possibility that Mum was gone for ever? Perhaps she should have used Mum's surname, and told the secretary she was Nina Flyte. Mum and Dad weren't married, so Mum's name was Miranda Flyte; she always put people right if they assumed she was Mrs Bickerstaff. Nina didn't blame her – she'd always thought that Miranda Flyte was a lovely name. It was just that Nina had always been Nina Bickerstaff at primary school; that was the name she was used to.

Why weren't Mum and Dad married, though? Nina had sometimes wondered, but now it seemed more important than ever. Was it a sign that Mum didn't want to bind herself to Nina and Dad, by sharing their name? That she'd always been planning to escape from them?

There were so many ifs and buts and maybes that Nina's head was swarming with them. As she walked away along the corridor, hoping she could find her way to the next lesson, she scowled at the floor, and aimed a kick at the skirting-board.

'What's up with you?' said a voice behind.

It was Cat, the girl from the bus. Caitlin Eagleton. Nina had seen her sitting at the front of the class in Geography. One of the last to enter the room, Nina had sat next to a very small boy who looked as if he belonged in primary school, and who seemed very anxious to get everything right. They hadn't exchanged a single word.

'Nothing,' Nina grumped.

'It's not that bad, is it?'

'You wouldn't know, would you?'

As soon as the words were out of her mouth, Nina

wished she could grab them back. Cat was the nearest thing she had to a friend in this huge, bewildering place.

'Sorry, I didn't mean—' Nina called, but Cat was already striding away fast. She'd done her hair differently today, in a thick plait, fastened high. Its tasselly end bounced on her shoulders as she walked, her whole body saying, *If you want to be a misery, that's up to you. I'm not letting you spoil my day.*

Now Nina felt even worse than before. The school day stretched in front of her like a marathon to be run – so many lessons, so many new classrooms to find, teachers' names to learn. How would she keep up? She couldn't concentrate for more than a moment. Her mind, now, was full of *Where's Dad?* as well as the *Where's Mum?* she was getting used to. Her mind came up with lurid plots. They'd planned this – to run off together, abandoning her. They were never coming back. They'd flown off to Australia, to start a new life without her . . .

Where was she supposed to be heading? She pulled out the planning diary she'd been given yesterday, and looked at the timetable pasted in at the back. Friday, period 3. Maths, Mrs Fisher, M62.

M62, to Nina, was the trans-Pennine motorway. She had a mental picture of the class sitting in a line on the hard shoulder, with a teacher trying to shout above the noise of zipping lorries.

She turned a corner, and came across Cat again, coming out of the girls' toilets. This time Cat looked straight at her without smiling, then turned away.

Nina scurried to catch up. 'I'm sorry! I didn't mean to be horrible.'

Cat shrugged. 'OK. Up to you.'

The way she said it, Nina wasn't sure whether she was forgiven or not. She tried again. 'The thing is …' But the busy corridor was no place for a conversation. People were shoving along in both directions, and Nina felt quite swamped by taller people with loud voices who nearly bashed her rucksack off her shoulder as they surged past. Then a bell shrilled, and at once the flow thinned as people filtered off left and right.

'We'd better hurry. My sister says this Maths teacher's really strict. It's this way, I think,' Cat said, turning left up a flight of stairs, which she climbed two at a time. Now the classrooms had names beginning with M for Maths, and M62 was the last one, at the end of the corridor.

The teacher, who was smiling now but looked as if she'd had years of practice at being cross, glanced up as they went in, and said, 'Quickly, please, girls. Two places there at the back. Be on time in future.'

Nina and Cat hurriedly sat down in the two spare seats, an aisle between them. As they both took out their things, Nina glanced at Cat's purple pencil case. It had a new adornment: a rosette, layers of fabric – some patterned, some plain – all in deep shades of blue and indigo, sewn into the shape of a huge flower, held together with a velvet-covered button in the middle. Nina stared at it.

'Where did you get that?'

'My sister got it for me yesterday. In this shop she goes to, Second—'

'My mum made it! It's all bits of her clothes and mine. She does lots of—'

'Young lady!' said a loud voice, directed her way. Nina froze, mouth still open. She hadn't even registered that the lesson was starting; Mrs Fisher stood by the whiteboard, looking like someone who expected no nonsense. 'The first thing you need to learn in my class is that no one speaks while I'm talking. What's your name?'

'Nina,' said Nina, shame-faced, and when Mrs Fisher tilted her head, expecting a fuller answer, she added, 'Nina Bickerstaff.'

At once she heard a whisper to her left: '*Flyte*-Bickerstaff, don't you mean, your ladyship?' and a whirlpool of suppressed giggles, too quiet for even the sharp-eared Mrs Fisher to hear.

❦

6

The Green Crocodile

—◆•◆•◆—

Nina couldn't take her eyes off the indigo rosette. It said *Mum* more loudly than she'd heard for days.

Last winter, Mum had had the idea of using fabric bits and pieces to make rosette brooches. Every one was different. Mum could never resist buying remnants of interesting fabric from the market, and sometimes, if she or Nina were discarding a garment too shabby for Second-Hand Rose, she'd cut it into pieces and use the best bits. She had a carrier bag full of scraps of velvet and cotton, gingham and brocade, coils of ribbon from presents. Mum wasn't particularly good at sewing, but when the television was on she liked having something to do with her hands. After she'd made the first two – one for herself, which she fastened to her red hat, and one for Nina to wear with her favourite denim jacket – she had the idea of giving them to the aunts to sell in the shop.

This particular one: Nina could remember Mum sewing it, while she was watching an old film one wet

Sunday afternoon in the summer holidays. It might even be the last one Mum had made. Nina could see a fragment of Mum's indigo velvet trousers – Mum had worn them so much that they'd gone threadbare at the knees and bum. And there was a piece from a purple checked shirt Nina had been wearing the time she fell out of the apple tree in Max's garden, ripping one of the sleeves. Three outer petals were made of corduroy, left over from elbow patches Mum had sewn on to Dad's old jacket.

That rosette said *Us*. It said *Family*. It said *The three of us. We belong together.*

'A-*hem!* Young lady in the back row!'

Nina had almost forgotten she was in the Maths lesson. Mrs Fisher was looking directly at her.

'Would you care to repeat what I just said?'

Nina could only gawp.

'I thought so,' said Mrs Fisher. 'First you were chatting, now not paying attention. *Not* a good start, Nina. You'll have to do better than this.'

Nina tried to tune in. Mrs Fisher was explaining the rules of a number puzzle; when she'd finished, she told the class to work at it in pairs. Nina looked across the aisle at Cat, but Cat had teamed up with the boy on her other side. The girl next to Nina was already staring at the numbers, head down over the paper hand-out, and didn't look as if she wanted any help.

At the end of the lesson, Mrs Fisher kept Nina back.

'Is everything all right? You didn't seem quite with us,' she said, in a kindlier tone than Nina expected.

'Yes. Yes, thank you.' Suddenly Nina was afraid she might cry. How awful would that be, blubbing like a baby in front of Mrs Fisher's next class? People big enough to be Year Tens or Elevens were clogging up the corridor, the keenest ones looking in through the open door.

Though unsure whether the conversation was finished, Nina turned away and pushed past them, wondering which way the Year Sevens had gone.

Today really wasn't going well.

❦

At the end of school, Nina looked for Cat on the bus, intending to be friendly. But Cat wasn't on the bus today, and Nina sat on her own again. She spent the whole journey sunk in gloom, hardly glancing out at the cloud-flecked moorland.

Her mood lifted as she got off at the marketplace and saw Max walking from the direction of the station, in the royal-blue blazer that was the uniform of Sir Frank Dalloway's. She needed to get him on Mum's case. Max loved puzzles of all kinds, the harder the better: chess problems, fiendish sudokus, crosswords, and detective stories that he devoured as soon as he could get his hands on them. One thing was for sure: once she got Max on the case, he wouldn't give up until Mum was found.

He swerved across the road to meet her. ''Lo, Neen. How's it going?'

'All right. You?'

'Yeah. Let's go to Fotheringay's.'

'OK, but I need to—'

'There's this cool chess set there.' Max was walking fast; Nina had to accelerate to keep up. She was fretting to tell him about Mum, but the street was too busy; she couldn't shout it out above the noise of traffic, for anyone to hear. It would have to wait.

Mr Fotheringay was the aunts' antique-dealer friend, who had a big shop just around the corner from Second-Hand Rose. The shop was full of dull antique stuff, but Max liked it because it also sold things like model armies and sometimes chess sets. Max loved chess. He'd organised the chess club at primary school, and had taught Nina to play, so she knew at least the basic moves even if she'd never ever *ever* be able to beat Max – only, once, when after six defeats he'd let her win, and she'd known, and was furious. That wasn't proper winning.

Mr Fotheringay was about the aunts' age, perhaps even older. He never seemed to be doing much when they went in: usually he was looking at a catalogue, or puzzling away at the cryptic crossword in *The Times*. He shared Max's love of chess, and sometimes they'd play a game together. For Mr Fotheringay, the pleasure was in handling the craftsman-made pieces, while for Max it was all about tactics and scheming.

Mr Fotheringay was at his desk now, head bent, not noticing Nina and Max as they gazed in from the street.

'See? Isn't it brilliant?' Max squatted down to look closely at a chess set in the window, which was otherwise full of boring plates, jugs and vases, footstools and boot-scrapers and Indian rugs. The chess pieces were set out ready for a game to start, with one pawn moved forward. The board was charcoal-grey and white, and the pieces were Gothic-looking: stern kings with long pointed beards, witchy queens, and castles with spindly turrets; the knights rode horses with proudly arched necks and flaring nostrils.

'How much d'you think it would cost?' Nina asked. Nothing in Mr Fotheringay's window ever had a price on it.

'I don't know. Hundreds, I bet. Thousands, even. Shall we go in?'

Nina followed him inside, hoping this wouldn't take long.

'Hello, young Max – hello, young Nina!'

Mr Fotheringay always seemed pleased to see them. Nina wondered how many customers actually came in; she rarely saw one. His shop wasn't nearly as busy as Second-Hand Rose.

'How's life treating you both?' He got creakily to his feet.

'Cool, thanks,' said Max.

'How are those excellent aunts of yours, Nina? They

haven't been to see me for a while. Tell your Aunt Rose to have a rummage about and find something to show me.'

'I will,' said Nina. The aunts came here if they had items to be valued; sometimes Mr Fotheringay would pay them quite well for a piece of bone china, a silver brooch or a piece of old lace. She wondered why he'd specified Aunt Rose, though. Aunt Nell was the one who prided herself on her sharp eye for something special.

'You've come to look at my Gothic chess set, I expect,' Mr Fotheringay said to Max. He moved across to the window, knelt down stiffly, and picked up two pieces. 'See? So unusual.' He handed a king to Max, a queen to Nina.

'Where did you get it?' Max asked.

'At an auction. It came in a beautiful box. May not have been out of it for years.' Mr Fotheringay looked hopefully at Max. 'It's a waste, isn't it? They want to be used. Got time for a game?'

Max dumped his rucksack on an upholstered chair, his face eager. 'Yeah! OK with you, Nina?'

'OK,' said Nina. She wanted Max to herself, but he'd be engrossed here for ages now. Carefully, Mr Fotheringay lifted the chessboard and its pieces to a low table; he pulled over a chair for himself, and gestured to Max and Nina to sit on the chaise longue. But Nina was too restless to sit. While the game began, she looked idly around the shop, her mind roaming elsewhere.

She checked her mobile. There was a text from Dad: **Hope 2day went well. I'm in Kendal. Talk later.**

Kendal! That was in the Lake District, Nina knew, or at least on the edge of it. Savitra, one of Mum's yoga friends, lived there; Nina remembered that she and her parents had stopped off to see her on their way to Coniston Water, last Easter holidays. Could Mum be staying there now? She loved the Lake District, that was for sure; she was always saying they should visit more often.

'I'd better go,' she said now, giving up on Max. 'The aunts are expecting me. Bye, Mr Fotheringay. See you at the weekend, Max?'

❦

Second-Hand Rose was busy this afternoon. A car was parked on the double yellow line, its boot open while a woman unloaded bin-bags. Inside, Aunt Nell was carrying the bags through to the storeroom, while Aunt Rose was talking to a customer who'd brought something back. From behind the changing-room door, a voice complained, 'I can't get into this at all – now the zip's stuck!' while a man waited patiently with a stack of books.

Sibyl, the Friday afternoon helper, was dithering by the window display. 'Hello, Nina,' she said, as the aunts were too busy to do more than nod. 'Where do you think I should put this?'

She held out the green crocodile. Nina stared at it, and the crocodile smirked back at her as if it knew something she didn't.

'With the toys, I suppose,' Nina said. 'Why doesn't someone *buy* it?'

'Perhaps it's a bit frightening for the children. I'll put it with the bric-a-brac. Someone might use it as a draught excluder.'

'A draught excluder!' exclaimed a woman searching through the ties. 'That's just what I need. Is this it? Well, it's different! How much?'

'Two pounds,' said Sibyl.

'I'll take it. Thanks.' The woman took the crocodile and joined the queue, behind the man with the books.

Nina felt sorry that the crocodile was going. She rather liked the gleam in its black button eyes, and its savage, knowing grin.

7

The Silver and Jet Cufflinks

Have a gd day, said Dad's Saturday morning text message. **Talk 2nite.**

Huh! *Have a good day* – and how, exactly, did he think that might happen? It could only be a good day if she made some kind of breakthrough.

Nina snapped her mobile shut and looked out of her attic window. More likely it would be Dad who made the breakthrough. He'd phoned last night to explain that he'd talked to Savitra but hadn't really found out anything useful, and was now off to Sheffield to meet another old friend of Mum's, called Alex. Alex? Who on earth was Alex? Nina didn't know Mum had a friend called Alex, or even whether it was a man Alex or a woman Alex. It made her feel uneasy, Mum having friends she knew nothing about.

And was Dad really planning to go from one place to another, everywhere Mum might have visited at some stage of her life? Where next? Sheffield didn't sound very hopeful – Mum didn't like cities. She liked small towns like Crowdenbridge, and she loved the moors. She liked the seaside – Robin Hood's Bay, and Whitby. Dad might as well try—

Brighton. The name slid into her mind, and a memory. She knew Mum liked Brighton. Max's brother was at Sussex University, and Max had sent a postcard when he went down to visit, at Easter. Nina had shown it to Mum, who said, 'Oh, lovely! I used to like going on the pier, after dark, when it was all lit up.'

But that was silly. Brighton was no more likely than Sheffield.

At least it was the weekend, and she'd have time to get on with things. The sun was shining, and it was market day, when the town would be busy with stalls and people. On any normal Saturday she'd go to the market with Mum, for fruit and veg and bread, and sometimes they'd go to Pumpernickel. On a *normal* Saturday ... *normal* was beginning to feel like a treacherous word, best avoided. What if she never knew *normal* again?

The phone played its message-incoming tune, and Nina flipped it open, her heart thumping. But it wasn't Mum; it was Max.

2moz TpWds, me ZMJ +U? 10

She was used to decoding Max's messages, and this sounded good: Tipton Woods, tomorrow, with Max's parents and his dog Zebedee. She sent back **Gr8!** – the aunts wouldn't mind, would they? – and got dressed, feeling quite optimistic. Her job for today was to search the entire shop and look for more clues – for anything Mum might have donated, intentionally or by mistake. She would tell Max everything tomorrow, by which time she hoped for clear Evidence. Max would be sure to ask for Evidence, and if there was anything in the shop, Nina intended to find it.

Just before nine, she walked with her aunts through the alleyway that led to the shop's back entrance. The front door, as Aunt Rose discovered when she went to unlock it from inside, was blocked by a barricade of overflowing boxes and bags.

'Tsk!' she went. 'I *do* wish people wouldn't do that. There's a big enough notice asking them not to leave things when we're closed.'

She opened the door, and a small avalanche toppled in; Nina went to help.

The aunts' treasure house: that was Mum's name for Second-Hand Rose. When she was younger, Nina couldn't see that at all. '*Treasure?* It's just a load of old clothes and china and stuff that people don't want.'

But Mum said that one person's cast-off was another person's treasure. 'You never know what might turn up. That's what makes it so fascinating.'

Nina thought about that now. She'd bought a few special things herself, and knew that Mum *had* found treasures – a hard-to-find yoga book, a floaty summer dress that had become her favourite after her old one got ripped – and maybe, now, she'd left some, too.

58

Maybe left things deliberately, for Nina to find – each one a clue, adding up to The Answer?

You never knew *who'd* come into the shop, either, but there were several people you could rely on. Today there'd be the knitting lady who came every Saturday, to buy oddments of wool that she knitted up into blanket squares for Africa. She must have knitted several square miles by now, Aunt Nell said, and Nina imagined a whole community of children sleeping snugly underneath a patchwork blanket the size of a country, with just a few faces and feet poking out at the edges. Then there'd be Mrs Freeman, who called regularly to update Aunt Rose with her latest visit to the doctor, every dizzy spell, every slight fluctuation in her health.

Nina started by looking through all the hanging-rails. Some of the clothes here were so horrendous that she couldn't imagine anyone buying them – a striped dress that looked like a deckchair, a sugar-pink blouse floppily frilled at neck and sleeves, a jacket the colour of horse dung, in fabric so hairy that she itched just looking at it. But there were gorgeous things too, and that was what always made it worth looking.

The door *ting*ed and a tall girl came in, the girl with striking fox-red hair. Today she wore a short denim skirt, scarlet tights, and a big, grey sweater. Pinned to the sweater was one of Mum's rosette brooches, like the one Nina had seen just yesterday on Cat's pencil case. Her hair was mostly tucked up into the trilby hat she'd bought on Thursday. She smiled at Nina as if she knew her, then went to the wooden box in the corner that held odds and ends of fabric.

'Hello again, dearie!' said Aunt Rose. 'Come back for more?'

'Yes,' said the girl.

The door *ting*ed again, and another girl came in – Cat, from school.

'And here's my sister,' said the taller girl.

'Oh, hi, Nina!' Cat wiggled her fingers in a sort of wave.

Of course! Nina should have guessed that the sister Cat had mentioned was the foxy-haired girl. They looked rather alike, now that she saw them together; they had different-coloured hair, but both liked wearing it in plaits and twirls, caught and gripped in interesting ways.

There were exclamations and introductions.

'What, do you work here? I didn't know!'

'Well, it's my aunts' shop.'

'*Is* it? Did you know that, Thea?' said Cat. 'Thea gets nearly all her clothes here – that skirt, and that sweater, and I've bought a few things, too—'

'Thea! What a lovely, unusual name!' exclaimed Aunt Rose. 'Is it short for Dorothea?'

'No, it's Theodora,' said Thea, 'but no one calls me that or I'd swipe them.'

'Well, you're certainly a good advert for our clothes,

dear!' Aunt Rose stood back to look her up and down. 'We ought to put you in the front window – don't you think, Nell?'

'Excuse me,' said a voice. 'I bought this yesterday to use as a draught excluder, but I'm bringing it back, I'm afraid. It's just too frightening for my little grandson. He cried and cried when he saw it, and wouldn't stop. No, I don't want a refund. I'll just give it back.'

It was the green crocodile. As the woman placed it on the counter, it seemed to look sidelong at Nina. There was something knowing and triumphant in its grin. Or maybe she was imagining it.

'Well, if you're sure,' said Aunt Nell. 'We've got plenty of nice toys. Why not find something your grandson will like?'

'You'll join in, won't you, Nina?' Cat was saying.

Nina must have missed something. 'Join in what?'

'The fashion show Thea's putting on at school, the week after next,' Cat explained.

'Anti-fashion, in a way,' said Thea.

'Everything's recycled, nothing new.' Cat waved an arm at the clothes rails and shoe racks. 'Jewellery, hats, shoes, belts – all from charity shops or car boot sales.'

'*Anti*-fashion?'

'Yes. Because fashion is all about making us want things we don't need,' said Thea. 'Buying stuff, spending money on whatever shops and magazines say is the next new thing. Do we all want to look the same as each

61

other, or what? Anti-fashion's much more interesting. More individual and a whole lot greener, as well. Using what we've already got. Giving clothes a new life.'

'When is it?'

'Thursday week. We've been planning it since last term,' said Thea. 'We have cake sales every week to raise the money, and then we spend it in charity shops, so everyone benefits.'

'Especially the people who eat the cakes,' added Cat. 'Nina can be in the show, can't she? I'm in it.'

'Course,' said Thea.

'Me? What, modelling? On a catwalk?'

'It's only putting clothes on and walking up and down,' said Thea. 'Up to you. You could help behind the scenes if you'd rather. And it's great that you're here so often. You could look out for the things I specially need. I'll write you a list.'

Nina was astonished at how readily she'd been accepted by Cat and Thea, made to feel part of their plans. 'OK. I'll definitely join in. Thanks!'

'Great, and thank *you*! Come to our meeting, Wednesday lunchtime. Cat's coming, aren't you, Cat?'

'What's this?' said Aunt Rose, transparently delighted that Nina had new friends. Any minute now she'd be offering fat rascals.

'Rose, there are customers waiting,' Aunt Nell told her. 'And we need more bags at the till.'

Another *ting* announced the arrival of Mrs Freeman.

She swept in, bringing a waft of perfume with her; over her arm she had two carrier bags from one of the town's smarter clothes shops. Nina saw the slightest upward roll of Aunt Nell's eyes, just the instant before she gave a welcoming smile. But Mrs Freeman homed in on Aunt Rose like a heat-seeking missile.

'Oh, there you are. I told you I've been back to the clinic? You'd laugh!' She had a way of picking up the conversation from her last visit – if it could be called a conversation, when Aunt Rose's part was merely to nod and shake her head, with the occasional 'No!' or 'Really?' or 'How awful!'

Mrs Freeman was quickly into her stride. 'The doctor said, "Well Mrs Freeman, we'd better take your blood pressure again, hadn't we?" And you'll never guess: it was higher than ever! I told him, it's all the stress, what with the double glazing and the dog's ringworm, not to mention the leaky stopcock. So he says, "Well, those pills don't seem to be working, we'd better try …"'

'Bags.' Aunt Nell held out her hand for them.

Aunt Rose passed them over the counter, her eyes never leaving Mrs Freeman's face. Nina watched, fascinated. Mrs Freeman was like a hypnotist, holding Aunt Rose in thrall. Thea and Cat had moved away to look at the hats; Aunt Nell, to show Aunt Rose that there were jobs to be done, was tidying the counter, jangling the dish of key-rings kept there, slapping down the Friends of the Hospital collecting box so fiercely that she startled a nearby customer into putting a coin through its slot.

Someone else had come in, a shy-looking woman with a little boy in tow. She didn't look at the things on display, but waited at the counter till Aunt Nell had served two customers. When it was her turn, she spoke so quietly that Nina – looking through the belts for something Thea might like – could barely hear.

'I bought this bag on Thursday, and when I got home I found some things in a pocket in the lining. I thought I'd better bring them back.'

'... so he says, "Well, Mrs Freeman, your heart rate's perfectly fine, no problem there ..."'

The shy woman held out a pair of silver-and-black cufflinks. 'They must have been left in there by mistake. Someone might come back, asking for them.'

'That's very good of you.' Aunt Nell held one of the cufflinks six inches from her nose, looking, Nina guessed, for a hallmark. 'Yes, that sort of thing does happen.'

'There were these, too.' The woman passed over a photograph and some sort of ticket. 'Quite old, by the look of them.'

Trying not to look nosy, Nina edged closer. On the counter was a small evening bag, made of a silky fabric in palest greeny-blue, sprinkled with seed pearls that winked sharp colours as they caught the light.

Nina stared, unable to look away. All at once there might have been nothing else in the shop but her and the bag. She was caught between a certainty that she'd never seen it before, and a strong feeling that it must have something to do with Mum. It was so exactly the sort of thing Mum liked; Mum would have bought it herself if she'd found it here.

Could this be the treasure she was looking for, the vital clue?

Aunt Nell put the photograph and the ticket in the drawer under the counter. 'I'll hang on to them just in case. Thank you!'

The woman smiled, and put the evening bag back into her shopper. 'This was such a good bargain – I didn't expect free gifts with it as well!'

'Oh, but—' Nina had to restrain herself from grabbing the bag back. Of course she couldn't. The woman had paid for it. It was hers now.

'What, dear?' said Aunt Nell.

Nina shrugged. 'Nothing.'

'Come on, Sammy,' said the young woman. 'We're going to the cake shop now.'

Nina watched as she left. What would Max say about letting a possible piece of Evidence walk out of the shop? It had gone, now, and she could hardly run down the street and demand it back. Still, the items in Aunt Nell's drawer might be Evidence too.

'Can I see the other things that were in the pocket?' she asked.

'It's only an old photograph,' Aunt Nell said, but took

it out, with the ticket. 'Two little boys. Twins, by the look of them.'

She showed Nina. Two smiling faces looked back at her: boys identically dressed in striped T-shirts and shorts, with cheeks so shiny that they might have been polished. They sat on a beach, side by side, holding big ice-cream cornets. She could see the concentration it took for them not to lick until their photo had been taken. Nice-looking boys: dark-haired, cheeky-faced, aged about five perhaps? Nina wasn't sure. Her spirits sagged. Just for a moment, she'd convinced herself that the photograph would be of Mum – though, even if it had been, how would that help? She *had* photos of Mum, plenty of them, downloaded on the computer at home. Photos couldn't reveal where she *was*.

'I don't know anyone with twin boys,' said Aunt Nell. 'Do you, Rose ... Rose?'

Aunt Rose was still pinned against the bookshelves, her eyes glazed, while Mrs Freeman continued, oblivious: '"No," I said, "I'm not traipsing up to the hospital just to sit for hours in that waiting room ..."'

'These are good cufflinks.' Aunt Nell was looking at them through a magnifying glass now. 'Hallmarked silver, and jet. Worth a bit. Rose,' she called, 'you can show these to your friend Mr Fotheringay. We may as well get them valued in case no one claims them.'

'*Our* friend, dear.' Rose managed a small aside, then

continued shaking her head and tutting. 'No, really, how awful ...'

'But hark at me, talking nineteen to the dozen.' Mrs Freeman sounded as if she might be finishing, at last. 'You don't want to listen to me all day, do you?'

Aunt Rose made a sound that could have meant several things, and seized the chance to extricate herself, stepping nimbly to the counter. 'Found anything, dears?' she said brightly to Thea and Cat.

'Yes, we'll take this fabric, and Cat found a nice beret and a belt,' Thea replied.

'What about that ticket?' Nina asked Aunt Nell, who picked it up from the counter.

'Just an old train ticket. French.' She put on her glasses to look more closely. 'Toulouse to Paris, single. Years old. No use to anyone.' Crushing it in her hand, she dropped it into the bin.

'Anyway – I'm due at the dentist.' Mrs Freeman gave a farewell wave to Aunt Rose, then sidled past the bric-a-brac and handed Aunt Nell twenty-five pence for the paperback she'd chosen from the Last Chance box – Nina's name for the reduced-price books that would go for pulping if no one bought them.

The door *ting*ed behind her. The shop felt suddenly quiet.

'At least she'll have to give her voice a rest, in the dentist's chair,' Aunt Nell muttered.

Aunt Rose pulled herself together like someone

67

blinking her way out of a trance. 'Right! What was I about to do?'

A man had come in as Mrs Freeman went out. 'Could someone give me a hand, please? I've got bags and boxes in my car, only I'm parked on a double yellow.'

Nina and Aunt Rose went out to help. As she carried a cardboard box into the shop, Nina heard giggles nearby, giggles that were beginning to sound all too familiar.

'Ooh, look, it's Lady Flyte-Bickerstaff!' Tash called across the street. 'Good morning, your ladyship! Isn't that a bit degrading, hanging out at a manky old charity shop?'

Manky! Nina might have raised a finger if she hadn't been clutching a heavy box with both hands. Instead, she gave them a pleasant smile. She wasn't going to let them wind her up, now that she was proper friends with Cat, and with Thea too, and was going to help with their show.

It felt like a good day, after all. A day full of promise.

8

The Bowl of Conkers

————◆•◆◆————

L ater, though, the doubts surged back. The fears.
The certainty that nothing would ever be the same
again.

Nina's trawl through the rails and racks didn't bring a
single extra clue to light. There were still bags and boxes
piled high in the storeroom, but surely anything brought
in by Dad would have been unpacked and sorted days
ago? All the same, Nina worked her way through dresses
and tea-towels, sweaters, books, cups and saucers and
toys, until her arms and eyes ached. She didn't want to
risk missing a Clue. So far, she only had the train ticket,
which she'd retrieved from the bin, just in case.

After lunch, she went out to look at the market.
Passing the flower stall, bright with chrysanthemums,
gladioli and lilies, Nina thought of Mum, and the last
time they'd been at the market together. On an impulse,
Mum had spent all her remaining cash on a big bunch
of her favourite cornflowers and anemones to put in a
jug on the kitchen table.

Impulsive. Yes, that was Mum.

Nina found herself thinking odd, disturbing thoughts. Who *was* Mum, really? It wasn't a question she'd ever considered. Always, she'd taken it for granted that Mum just *was*; not always the same, no, you couldn't say that about Mum, but at least always Mummish in her own unpredictable, excitable ways. Now that Nina thought about it, she really didn't know much about Mum as a girl: Mum when she was Nina's age now, or when she'd been thirteen, or sixteen, or eighteen. She knew that her parents had met at a theatre in Bradford, where Dad had been stage carpenter, and Mum had been a dancer and choreographer. Mum had been a dancer when she was younger; Nina did know that.

She sometimes wondered how she and Mum could be so different – Mum light on her feet, slim and agile, Nina strong and sturdy, without a musical instinct in her body. Dad said she'd inherited that from him; tone deaf, he said he was, as well as flat-footed. But Mum delighted in movement. She would improvise ballet steps while she folded sheets from the washing-line, stand gracefully on one leg while she drained the pasta, twirl around lamp posts like someone in an old musical. Dance ran through her veins, Dad said.

'So why don't you dance any more?' Nina sometimes asked her. 'I mean, you know, like in shows?'

'Oh, that was fine when I was younger,' Mum would say, as if she were bent and wrinkly now. 'I've got enough

70

to do without all those rehearsals and hanging about.'

'Were you *famous* when you were a dancer?'

'No! Not the slightest bit.' Mum would give her funny half-smile. 'Most dancers aren't famous, you know. It's just a job.'

Still, it felt *glamorous* to have a mum who'd been a dancer, and who looked as if she could be one still. When Nina had been young enough to have Mum collect her from school, she'd felt proud as she'd looked towards the playground railings where other mums and a few dads waited with toddlers and buggies. Other mums looked ordinary; hers was special. Different. As if being a mum was something she managed to fit in around her far more exciting life . . .

But, now, that thought didn't feel comfortable at all.

Nina entertained the idea that Mum had gone back to the stage. What if she'd been head-hunted for the lead role in a dance production in London, maybe even in New York, on Broadway? She saw Mum looking young and beautiful in stage make-up and a clingy, gem-studded dress, receiving the cheers of an adoring audience, accepting a huge sheaf of flowers . . .

No. Mum wouldn't just *go.*

But what was the use of thinking that? Mum *had* gone, hadn't she?

Nina looked at the other market stalls without much interest, wishing Max wasn't busy today, playing in a chess tournament as he often did on Saturdays. She

71

trailed around, thinking that she might as well go back to the shop, but then her stride quickened, and she found herself walking towards Royds Row. Her own street. Home.

It wasn't a very special sort of house when you looked at it from outside. It was small and narrow, with a front door that opened straight on to the pavement. There was a nice curly knocker that twirled into the shape of a fish, but that and the blue paint on the door and window sills were the only things that made this house look any different from the nine others in the terrace.

It was only when you went inside that you knew it was Home, and Nina hadn't got a key of her own. She did the best she could, which was to stand at the window and peer into the front room.

There was the fireplace, with its patterned tiles. There were the bookshelves either side, crammed to overflowing. There was the rug with a burnt patch, where the fire – Mum refused to change it for a gas one – had spat out a piece of smouldering wood. There was the sofa with its saggy cushions, covered with an Indian throw that hid the threadbare bits. There was the door through to the kitchen, giving a glimpse of the cork notice board where they all pinned things like tokens and leaflets, or just pictures and postcards they liked.

It had been Mum's birthday just over a fortnight ago, and the cards were still on the mantelpiece. In the centre was the small turquoise bowl Nina had bought for her at Second-Hand Rose, which had conkers in it. Nina could never resist picking up new conkers, so glossy and richly coloured, especially when they were still in their spiky shells, showing themselves to perfection against the pale lining. The turquoise bowl had seemed the obvious place to put them.

'Better than jewels, they are,' Mum had said. And the bowl itself was beautiful, a deep and vibrant greeny-blue with a pearlescent glaze, the colours shifting and changing as you turned it in your hand. It was a Treasure.

Nina's nose was pressed flat against the glass, and beginning to feel numb.

The house looked so different with no one in it, the air undisturbed for nearly two whole days. It needed voices and music and feet clomping up the stairs to bring it to life. The house missed them, she knew; Mum and Dad and herself, absent as ghosts.

What if no one came back, ever? What if the house stayed empty for always, and Nina could only peep in, like a burglar? She was starting to feel like a stalker – stalking her own life, behaving furtively, as if she had no right to be here. Already she felt like a different Nina, sadder and lonelier than the one who'd been here ten days ago, the Nina whose house this was. The Nina who had a mum.

'What's up, dear?' said a voice. 'Locked yourself out?'

It was Mrs Enderby, creeping slowly along the street

with the tartan trolley she used more for support than for shopping. Often it contained just the local paper, or a carton of milk.

'No, not really.' Nina stepped back from the window.

'I hear your mum's gone on a little holiday. Anywhere nice?'

'Oh – yes, thank you. Somewhere lovely. It was a surprise,' Nina said.

Well, that last bit was true. Not wanting to explain, she said goodbye, and hurried back to the market square before she could meet any more neighbours.

❧

Later that evening, Nina brooded on this. Were people gossiping about Mum? Did they know Dad had gone, too? Were they seeing Nina as a poor little waif, abandoned by both parents, shut out of her home?

No one could feel waif-like at the aunts' house. Uncle Derek cooked a big dinner; he liked cooking, especially on a Saturday evening. Afterwards, he and the aunts watched an old film on TV, or supposedly watched it, but before long they'd all nodded off, with Nina the only person left awake. Their film finished, and was followed by a chat show, but they all dozed on, Aunt Rose snoring softly.

Nina had been trying to read, but couldn't concentrate. She put her book down quietly, so as not to disturb the sleepers; she crept up to her bedroom, the best place for a mobile signal, and found a new message from Mum.

Be a good girl for your aunts. Love you lots. Mum xxx

So Mum *knew*! Did that mean she'd been talking to Dad, actually talking? No, probably not. Dad must have sent a text message. But how did Mum have the nerve to talk about being good?

Nina tried the number. Voicemail. Of course. She might as well give up the idea that Mum would ever *answer.*

'Mum?' There was an accusing note in Nina's voice. 'You know Dad's gone after you? But he really doesn't know where to start. Are you coming home soon? Are you coming home *ever*?'

Still, this was something to tell Max: that Mum and Dad were definitely in touch. Only now did she remember that she hadn't told the aunts about going out with Max tomorrow. As she ran down to ask if it would be OK, the phone rang, startling her aunts out of their slumbers. Aunt Rose nodded and blinked with a guilty look; Aunt Nell opened her eyes perfectly calmly; Uncle Derek carried on sleeping. It was Aunt Nell who got up to answer.

'Richard! Yes, Nina's here. Where are you? Yes, yes. Here she is.'

Nina took the phone.

Dad's voice seemed to come from a long way off.

'How are you, precious? What have you been doing today?'

Nina gave brief answers, then: 'Never mind about me. I'm fine. What about you? Are you staying with this Alex person? What have you found out?'

'I'm still in Sheffield, yes, heading off tomorrow. I've got more people to meet, then I'll probably head south.'

This all sounded hopelessly vague – as if he was a bird, about to migrate to a warmer climate.

'But who *are* all these people? Why couldn't you have just emailed them, or phoned?'

'I thought . . .' Dad sounded less sure of himself now. '. . . someone might have heard something – might remember something. It's easier face to face.'

'And south – *where* south? D'you mean Brighton?'

'Brighton? Why Brighton?'

'Just an idea. Mum likes Brighton.'

'I didn't know she'd ever been there,' said Dad.

'Oh, yes, she's definitely been there. She said.'

'Did she?' There was doubt in Dad's voice now. 'Well, maybe I will. Just give me a bit longer. I know this is hard for you, precious – but trust me, I'll be back as soon as I can.'

'With Mum?'

'With Mum,' Dad repeated, but with a wavering note in his voice that sounded as if he couldn't convince himself, let alone Nina. He asked more questions about school, about helping in the shop, about her Saturday, then asked to be handed back to Aunt Nell. 'I'll phone again tomorrow evening. I promise.'

The conversation with Aunt Nell, the half Nina could hear, went: 'But what are you – How – Who's – Hmm. Hmm. Hmmmmm. Yes, I see. If you say so.'

'What did he say?' Aunt Rose asked, when the call was finished.

'Well, he seems to have a few ideas,' Aunt Nell said brightly. 'But will they lead anywhere? I do wonder about all this driving round the country. Not to mention all the work he must be putting on hold.'

'Oh, I do hope he'll find her!' Aunt Rose, on her feet now, enveloped Nina in a big hug. 'Poor darling, poor sweetheart. Such a worry for you. So unsettling.'

Nina had noticed that her aunts rarely mentioned Mum. They talked about Richard, about Nina, and often – in Aunt Rose's case – about how awful she must be feeling, but it seemed that Mum had become *unmentionable*, as if she'd done something so awful that they were pretending she didn't exist.

Aunt Rose rubbed Nina's back. She had a way of making Nina feel like an invalid, when in fact Nina was now full of energy, keen to *do* something instead of sitting about moping.

'It's all right if I go out with Max tomorrow, isn't it?' she asked. 'With his mum and dad, to Tipton Woods? They usually take a picnic when they go out walking, so I won't be back till tea time.'

'Lovely!' beamed Aunt Rose. 'Yes, get a bit of fresh air in your lungs.'

'Of course you can,' said Aunt Nell. 'Good idea. Now, I think it's time for hot chocolate.'

Aunt Rose was yawning as she followed her sister down the kitchen stairs. 'Good film, wasn't it? I do enjoy a good film.'

Left alone with just the sleeping Uncle Derek for company, Nina found herself wondering why on earth she'd thought Dad should try Brighton. She frowned with the effort of remembering exactly what Mum had said, that time, looking at the postcard. The pier, yes, and something about shopping streets called The Lanes, and having a picnic up on the Downs. It sounded as if she'd spent a lot of time there, but when Dad came in, and Nina showed him and said, 'Could *we* go to Brighton, one day?' Mum's only comment had been that Brighton was a busy place, full of tourists, and that the east coast was much nearer.

It was as if she'd suddenly pretended not to like Brighton after all. As if it were just a place she'd heard about, not a place she *knew*.

Tomorrow Nina would tell Max everything. She thought of Tipton Woods, and splashing through the stream; then she remembered that her walking boots were at home. She went down the kitchen stairs to ask her aunts if they had a door key.

Halfway down she stopped dead, flattening herself

against the wall so that they wouldn't see her. They were talking together in low voices. Talking about *Mum.*

'What can she be thinking?' Aunt Rose's voice was an indignant whisper. 'Whatever's happened, it can't be good enough reason to desert Richard and Nina like this. Just when Nina's starting her new school, poor little mite. I can't begin to *imagine* ...'

'Well, that's Miranda for you,' Aunt Nell said. 'Always was a flighty piece if you ask me. Flyte by name, flighty by nature – not a grain of common sense in her head. Thank goodness Richard's got both feet squarely on the ground. And Nina seems to take after him, which is just as well.'

The next bits were drowned in rummaging sounds and the clatter of saucepans, but then Nina heard the *phut* of the gas stove, and her aunts were audible again.

'What if she's – you know – *gone off* with someone? I mean, you know, with another man?' Aunt Rose suggested.

A *hmmph* from Aunt Nell. 'Wouldn't surprise me. Wouldn't surprise me one bit. Doesn't know when she's well off, that one. Head in the clouds.'

'But then, why wouldn't she *say*? Why all this mystery?'

'This is Miranda we're talking about, remember. Used to be on the stage. Loves the theatre. Loves a bit of drama. And here she is, creating a drama of her own.'

'But what if she—'

'Never a thought for anyone else. And Richard,

chasing after her … Best leave her to her own devices, I'd have thought. She'll turn up when it suits her.'

'Well, I do hope so. I really, really do.'

'As for whether Richard ought to take her back when she *does* roll up – well, he will, of course. But I wonder if she deserves it. I wonder if she deserves *him.*'

Nina's heart was thumping. She stood with the palms of both hands flat against the wall, as if she might fall over otherwise. She judged from the tinkling of spoon against mug that the hot chocolate was nearly ready, and that her aunts would climb the stairs at any moment. Very cautiously, on tiptoes, she mounted the steps and went back to the sitting room, where Uncle Derek, fully awake now, was watching the news. Nina watched, too, not taking in a single thing, her head full of what she'd just heard.

It didn't sound as if the aunts liked Mum much at all! They were siding with Dad, against Mum. Nina didn't want to think of her parents as being on different sides, and she was quite sure Dad didn't think like that, either.

What else did they say, when she wasn't listening?

The mum they talked about – selfish, scheming, unreliable – didn't sound much like the mum Nina knew. She *liked* the way Mum was, and didn't want her any different. At least, different only in one way. It would be nice to have a mum who stayed. A mum who answered her phone. A mum who was where she ought to be, where you could find her.

'What if she's – you know – gone off with someone? Another man?' Aunt Rose had wondered, and Aunt Nell had said she wouldn't be surprised. That was what had shocked Nina most of all.

Mum? Mum wouldn't do that!

Nina knew that grown-ups sometimes did that sort of thing – Millie Adams's dad, for one – but not *Mum.* Not unless she'd been planning in secret for ages. Meeting someone. Pretending things were normal. Telling lies.

No. Not Mum.

But the thought sneaked into Nina's head that Mum had all sorts of chances to meet people – at the dance studio or in her classes, or at the Co-op. Mum was lively and pretty, and looked younger than she was. Of course people would like her. Admire her.

But that didn't necessarily mean ... Did it?

A picture began to form in Nina's mind of some horrible handsome man, smarmy and flattering, buying Mum presents and flowers, trying to lure her away. Had there *been* any unexplained flowers? Any mysterious bouquets? There had definitely been flowers for Mum's birthday, and not from Dad ... Nina remembered because they were big flamboyant lilies, and Dad couldn't stand the smell of them. Who had sent them? Surely Mum must have said ...

Could this be a Clue? If so, it wasn't one that Nina liked much, but she stored it in her memory with the others.

'Here's your hot chocolate, dear,' said Aunt Nell, handing her a steaming mug. 'And then I think it's your bedtime.'

Climbing the stairs to her attic room, Nina felt lonely. She was the only one here who really cared about Mum. It made her all the more determined to find out where she was.

9

The Jewelled Evening Purse

———◆•◆•◆———

U p in the woods, with Max and his parents, and Zebedee the black Labrador bounding ahead, Nina felt energised. Free. More herself than she'd felt for days.

The woods followed the course of a narrow river, with paths that wound between rocks and over gnarly tree-roots, leading right up to the open moor. It was windy today, windy and grey. The tree canopies were tossed and shaken, and all the time there was the rush of water; sometimes so close that Zebedee could dash into it, showering everyone with spray; sometimes so far below, as the path led over high crags, that Nina felt giddy if she looked down.

There was a main track, well-trodden by walkers' feet, but Max and Nina always chose a steep, rocky alternative if there was one, even if it meant getting snagged by brambles and ducking under branches. In places they could leap across the stream and back again. Once, ploshing in, Nina got her trainers soaked – she'd forgotten all about her walking boots until it was too late to go and fetch them. Aunt Nell and especially Aunt Rose would have constantly told her to be careful, but Max's parents took the view that she and Max were sensible enough to look after themselves, and left them to it.

This was Nina's chance, between scrambling over rocks and puffing up the steep bits, to tell Max about Mum. As she'd expected, he was immediately interested – not in a particularly sympathetic way, but that didn't matter, because what she wanted was not sympathy but ideas. At once, he asked lots of practical questions she hadn't thought of.

'How much money did she have with her? Has she got her own bank account, or does she share one with your dad? Because if they share one, he can go online and see if she's drawn any cash out. If she has, he could find out where.'

'I don't know. I'll ask him.'

Nina could almost see Max's brain firing up with enthusiasm for his new project.

'Did she take out lots of cash just before she went? Or buy any tickets with her card? What about the people at the Co-op? Did she have friends there?'

They jogged and panted their way up the final slope, where the path flattened and came out from the trees to open sky. Zebedee rushed ahead, barking joyfully. It always surprised Nina how *big* the sky was up here.

It made her feel small, standing underneath it, high enough for the wind almost to lift her off her feet and carry her away. Crowdenbridge was quite hidden, deep in the folds of the valley. You couldn't see any houses or buildings at all, though Nina knew that the path led to a farm in the dip between hills. The moor belonged to the sheep and the birds and the wild animals, disturbed only by occasional walkers. It made her feel strong and capable to know that her own legs and feet had brought her so far, and could take her a long way farther yet.

Marcus and Jo (Max always called his parents by their first names, and they'd told Nina to do the same, though it never felt quite right) caught up more slowly, looking round for a sheltered place to sit and eat their picnic lunch.

'Don't tell them about this,' Nina whispered to Max. She wasn't sure why, but she wanted to pretend that everything was normal.

Later, at Max's house, it was time to write things down and be orderly.

What Nina liked best about this house was its big cellar, furnished as a sitting room or TV room. Max's parents liked listening to music in the evenings, so if Max wanted to watch television or use the computer he came down here. His chessboard had its own low table, with the pieces set up ready, in case he could lure his mum or dad down for a game. There was a long, squashy sofa, and chairs made of cane. It felt odd to

Nina to be in a room with no windows, but it was a great place for planning and plotting, because anyone interrupting would have to clomp down the wooden stairs.

Max sat at the desk with a pen and notebook, and Nina sank into the beanbag nearby, her favourite sitting-place. It was also the favourite seat of Orlando, the black cat, but he didn't mind sharing.

'So.' Max wrote NINA'S MUM as the heading. 'Let's make a list of everything we know. Your mum did her yoga class on the Friday. That was Friday a week ago – umm – the second of September. And later that day, she left. But what about earlier that week? When did she start clearing out her stuff?'

He was making a list, writing the dates backwards: *Thursday 1st September, Wednesday August 31st.*

'I don't know when she started. I didn't see her doing it. But it was Wednesday or Thursday when Dad took the boxes to the shop.'

'And she left a note? What did it say? Can you remember the exact words?'

Nina could. 'It said *Gone away for a while. Don't worry. Love you both very much. Miranda.* And kisses, ten of them. You know, x for a kiss.'

Max wrote this down in his quick scratchy handwriting.

'And when did she send the first text?'

'Next day, Saturday. She sent it to Dad. It just said *Don't worry. I'll be back, but not yet.*'

Max noted that. 'So, has your dad tried phoning?'

'Yes, course he has. So have I. But she never answers.'

'And the next text?'

'She sent one to me. It said ... It said ...'

'Yes?' Max was waiting, pen poised.

Nina took her mobile out of her pocket, found the message and showed it to him.

'*Love you – see you soon,*' he read aloud, then wrote it down.

Nina's eyes filled with tears. Her lower lip trembled. The words sounded flat and meaningless in Max's voice, as empty as they'd seemed each time she'd looked at them over the last days, which was often. Quickly, she snapped the mobile shut and tucked it into her pocket. A tear slid from her eye and she brushed it away, hoping Max hadn't noticed, but he had.

'Oh, look, don't cry.' He was as embarrassed as she was. 'Crying won't help. We're doing something, aren't we? We'll solve it. Don't worry. She keeps saying she'll come back, so I bet she will. Why wouldn't she?'

'It's just ...' Nina sniffed, and groped in her other pocket for a tissue. 'Those words – what do they mean? If she really ...'

If she really loved me, if she really loved me and Dad, she wouldn't go off and leave us. But she couldn't risk saying those words, or she'd start sobbing and not be able to stop, and Max would hate that even more than she would. She blinked fast, making herself concentrate on facts. Facts were what Max liked.

Ten minutes later, after a lot of questioning and double-checking, Max had completed his list of Known Facts and Dates.

'So. Who sent the birthday flowers? That needs sorting out. Then the clear-out, the things that went to the shop. There must be a clue there. We'll make a list of those, next.'

'The thing is,' Nina said, still a bit snuffly, 'I'm not sure exactly what *was* Mum's.'

After a few moments of thinking and writing, Max's list read:

> *Elephant Bag (Nina has it)*
> *Scarf with bird pattern (bought by Thea Eagleton,*
>   *sister of Cat in Nina's class)*
> *China seahorse, bought by the aunts*
> *Rosettes, made specially for shop, two bought by Thea*
>   *– 1 for Cat*
>   *– 1 for self*

'Is that it, then?' Max said, looking up.

It didn't seem much.

'Well, like I said,' Nina told him, 'there might be things of Mum's still in the shop, only I haven't seen them. And things that have been sold – I won't ever see those. But where does this get us? Mum sent things to the shop – that doesn't tell us where *she* is.'

'No, but I wish we knew why she had the big clear-out.'

'Because Dad made new shelves. That's what he said.'

'Yes.' Max tapped his front teeth with the top of his pen. 'But people often have reasons, I mean, really deep reasons, for keeping shed-loads of stuff they don't need but can't throw out. I've seen TV programmes – my mum likes them. The people nearly always end up crying, and then feeling better. It always means something.'

'But *what?*'

'For the people on TV, it's usually something from the past that's upset them.'

Nina thought about this, then burst out, 'Oh, but that's silly! It wasn't like Mum had cupboards and cupboards full. She didn't have *shed-loads*. She just put out a few things she doesn't need any more. Everyone does that.'

'OK, but most people don't chuck out stuff and disappear a few days later. The bits and pieces she threw out might tell us what was on her mind. Are you saying there's no link?'

Nina looked down. It was a comfort to have the cat snuggled against her. A purring cat could make anything seem better.

'Now,' Max went on, 'are you quite sure there wasn't anything else?'

He was looking at her so intently that she thought she'd better come up with something. There was the jewel-scattered evening bag, and the feeling she'd had about it.

'There was a beady evening bag. Just yesterday. Small, like a kind of purse, made of silky stuff. A woman, youngish, brought it back because she'd found some things inside. There were cufflinks – she thought they might be valuable. Aunt Nell thought so, too. She wanted to show Mr Fotheringay. And there was a photo of twin boys in it, as well.'

'How old? What were they like?'

Nina described them, and Max wrote everything down.

'And a train ticket. Toulouse to Paris,' Nina added. 'I've got that.'

'Neen,' Max said excitedly, 'these are the best clues yet. Why didn't we have them on the list?'

'Because ...' Nina was shamefaced now. '... The ticket was from years ago. And I don't know that the bag belonged to Mum. I mean, it *might* have, but it probably didn't.'

With a muffled sound of frustration, Max flung his pen to the floor, where it rolled out of sight. 'Duh! I can't make a list of every single thing in the shop, just in case it belonged to your mum.'

'I just thought it was interesting, that's all.'

'OK.' Max had to lie face-down on the carpet and

reach under the desk to retrieve his pen. 'So we've listed everything that *was* your mum's? You haven't forgotten anything?'

Nina shook her head.

'Keep your eyes open from now on,' Max said, turning to a new page.

'Duh!' Nina went, because she hated it when Max said that to her. 'You think I've been walking around with them tight shut?'

'You might easily have missed something. I'm not saying it's your *fault*. You're always busy when you're in that shop. I know you said all your mum's stuff would have been unpacked by now, but there might be something that got stuffed in a corner, or missed somehow. See if you can look at everything. Text me when you've done it.'

Nina agreed, and they both fell silent: Nina stroking Orlando and feeling the deep, growly rumble of his purr; Max gazing at nothing.

After a few moments, Max said, 'I've got an idea.'

'Yes?'

'In crime stories, the person they're looking for always turns out to be right there under their noses.'

'What's that got to do with it? Mum's not a criminal, and this isn't a story!'

'No, but listen. What if your mum hasn't actually gone anywhere?'

Nina made a *kkk* sound. 'And how would that make

sense? You think she's been hiding at home, and Dad and I haven't noticed?'

'Just a thought. But what if ...' A look of revelation crossed Max's face; he snapped his fingers and sat upright. 'Your mum's into yoga and meditation and all that kind of stuff, isn't she? Where would she go, if she wanted to get away from everything?'

'To her bedroom?'

'I don't mean her bedroom. There are special places, aren't there? You know, *retreats*, where you can have your head massaged and live on herbal tea and seaweed. You can get up at three in the morning and walk about in bare feet, and sit cross-legged on the floor, chanting.'

'Mum would love that,' said Nina, imagining it. 'Where *are* these places?'

Footsteps sounded at the top of the stairs. 'All right down there, you two?' called Max's mum.

'Jo!' Max shouted back. 'We need your help for a minute.'

Max's mum came all the way down. 'I was just going to ask if you'd like to stay for tea, Nina. I can drive you back afterwards.'

'Thanks! I'd love to, but I'd better ring my—' Nina stopped abruptly, not wanting to explain. 'I'd better ring home,' she finished, then felt bad because she'd said *home* for her aunts' house, instead of her real home.

'Where would you go if you wanted to get away from everything?' Max asked his mum.

'Antarctica,' said Jo, leaning against the stair-post.

'Not Antarctica. I mean somewhere close to here. Just for a weekend, or a few days. Somewhere you could, you know, relax and be looked after and drink prune juice.'

'A spa break, you mean?' She looked puzzled. 'Why on earth are you interested in those? You can't tell me you're feeling the stress of school, after just two days.'

'It's not for me. It's a hypothetical question,' Max said. 'We were just wondering.'

'Hmm. Let me think. There's Millthorpe Health Spa, the other side of Hattersfield. Very expensive. You can go there for mud treatments and hot stone therapy and facials. Not my sort of place at all. If I wanted to stay somewhere really quiet, I'd go to a monastery.'

'A monastery? Can you do that? I mean, do they let ordinary people in?'

'Oh, yes, some do. You can join in the prayers and services, or just *be* there and enjoy the quiet and the routines. There's one at Lumberforth. It's not that far away.'

'Oh!' said Nina. 'Yes. There are leaflets at Tiffany's studio. I've seen them in the rack, in reception. But I didn't know it was a monastery.'

Max wrote down the name; his mother watched him curiously. 'Well, do let me know if you'd like me to book you a monastic retreat. Tea in half an hour. D'you want to use the phone, Nina?'

Nina said that she had her mobile, and Jo went back upstairs.

'That's it!' Max was perched on the edge of his seat, ready to spring into action. 'It all adds up.'

'Does it?' Nina didn't quite see how.

'Course! Your mum's gone in search of a simple life. It all makes sense. You just said there are leaflets at the yoga place. She's staying at the monastery for a bit.'

'Yes, but why wouldn't she—'

'See, it all fits! She's been giving away her favourite things – that's what you do if you want to be a monk. Monks don't need as much stuff as we've all got.'

Nina gave him a *duh* look. 'You're saying Mum wants to be a monk? That's just bonkers!'

'No, course not,' Max huffed, 'but you can't tell me she's not into hippy stuff like that. Yoga. Vegetarian food. Meditating. I bet you anything that's where she's gone.'

'But why wouldn't she *tell* us?'

'It's all part of the retreat thing, I s'pose. Cutting yourself off from the outside world. Well, what now?' Max looked at her. 'We could just wait and see if she comes back. Or we could get out there and find her!'

❧

10

The Map of Toulouse

———◆•◆———

When Dad phoned that night, Nina considered telling him Max's theory, but decided not to. Only Max could make the idea sound at all convincing. Dad was in Sussex now, anyway, miles from Lumberforth. At the suggestion of Alex, he was on his way to visit Clare, another of Mum's long-ago friends.

'Then I thought I'd head down to Brighton.'

'What,' said Nina, awed, 'just because I said?'

'There's nothing to lose.'

Nina had stopped thinking that Brighton could possibly be significant, but at least she knew where Dad would be when she wanted him back. Wouldn't it be great to surprise him by producing Mum? 'Dad, come home,' she imagined herself saying. 'Mum's not in Kendal or Sheffield or Brighton. She's here.'

Instead, she came out with, 'Dad. Why aren't you and Mum married?'

There was a silence so long that she thought she'd

been cut off. Then Dad said, 'It just didn't happen, precious. It wasn't that ...'

Nina waited, then prompted, 'Didn't you ask her?'

'Yes, I did. More than once. It was Mum who didn't want to.'

'Why not? Doesn't she love you?'

'Yes, she ... she said she did.' Nina heard him sigh. 'Does, I mean. Does. It's just ...'

'What?'

'You know what Mum's like. She doesn't want to be the same as everyone else. She couldn't see any point in being married. "It's only a piece of paper," she said. "We don't need it to prove we ..."' There was a catch in his voice. '"... We love each other." And we do, Nina. We do love each other. And we love you. Don't ever forget that.'

If he carried on like this, Nina would start blubbing again, as if the tears she'd fought back at Max's house were still there, waiting to be spilled. To divert them, she asked, 'You know those birthday flowers Mum got? The florist delivered them?'

'The stinky lilies?'

'Mm. D'you know who sent them?'

'Yes,' said Dad. 'It was the girls from the Co-op. There was a card.'

An ordinary explanation! Not a great mystery after all, not a secret man – only the 'girls' Mum worked with. Mum always teased Dad for calling them that,

96

when most were women in their forties and fifties.

'Who's this Clare, then, Dad? What have you found out?'

'Oh – each person I talk to gives me the name of someone else. They're all leads. Eventually I'll get to the one person who knows.'

Later, in bed, Nina couldn't sleep; her mind was buzzing with ideas and worries that circled like hornets. She thought of something else she wished she'd asked. *Why am I an only child? Why haven't I got a brother or a sister?*

Nearly everyone she knew had brothers or sisters. Max had a much older brother, away at university. Cat had Thea. The aunts had each other. Hannah from Mrs Grace's class had a new baby brother, on whom she doted. Nina had sometimes wondered if that might happen to her; Mum might have another baby. It wasn't too late, was it?

At least, it *hadn't* been too late. Not until Mum had cut herself adrift.

❦

'I'm really glad you're going to be in the fashion show,' Cat said, in the break-time queue on Monday. 'I was going to be the only Year Seven, but now there'll be two of us.'

'In it? Am I really?' Nina had almost forgotten, in her worry about Mum.

'Well, course,' said Cat. 'If you want to, that is.'

97

'Course – I wouldn't miss it for anything! Thank you.'

Cat struck a modellish pose. 'Thea's already found clothes for me, and she'll soon have something for you. She's brilliant at finding just the right things, you'll see. It'll be fun, won't it?'

'Yes, I ...'

'Nee–na!' went a voice behind her, and a second joined in, wailing like a police siren. 'Nee–na! Nee–na!'

Jem and Tash. Tiring at last of their Lady Flyte-Bickerstaff joke, they'd found a new one.

'Very funny,' Nina retorted. 'If you were five years old.'

'Hilarious,' added Cat.

Tash raised her hands, her fingers curled over like claws. 'Miaow, miaow.'

'Poor little Nee-na,' Jem said, in a voice full of fake sympathy. 'Is it true your mum's left – gone off with another bloke? That's what my gran says.'

'*What* did you say?' Nina's voice came out as a yip. 'What's it got to do with your gran?'

'She lives in your street,' Jem said smugly. 'Betty, her name is. Really she's my *great*-gran. Betty Enderby.'

Mrs Enderby! Nina felt herself goggling, and immediately tried to stop, because that was exactly what Jem wanted. Mrs Enderby, with her tartan shopping-trolley! A neighbour, almost a friend to Mum and Dad – she used to babysit, sometimes, when Nina was little

– and now she was gossiping about Mum! Making up lies, even—

'Well, that shows how much *she* knows. It's rubbish!' Nina retorted. She paid for her orange juice and muffin, and followed Cat, in what she hoped was a dignified manner, to a bench at the side of the canteen.

'What was that all about?' Cat asked.

Nina hadn't intended to tell Cat about Mum's disappearance – not yet, anyway – but moments later it had all spilled out.

'She wouldn't go off with anyone. She'd *never* do that.' She darted an angry look at Jem, who was with Tash by the door, flirting with a group of Year Nine boys.

'That sort of thing does happen, though,' Cat said. 'A lot. You can't always tell. My dad, for a start. He left my mum three years ago, when he met Polly.'

'Oh,' Nina said flatly. It was hard to know what to say.

'It's what they're like, adults. They pretend they're all sensible and responsible. Then they go and do something like that.'

'And did he come back?'

'No.' Cat polished an apple on her sleeve. 'It's OK. It was awful at first, but you get used to it.'

'Do you?'

Cat nodded. 'They're married now, him and Polly. They've got a little boy. And Mum's got a nice boyfriend called Bill. He stays over at weekends. Thea and I see our dad quite a lot. He lives in Manchester.' She flipped

99

open her phone and showed Nina a photo of a smiling toddler. 'Look, here's Flynn, my half-brother. He's gorgeous!'

Nina took a bite of her muffin, taken aback at the speed of this. Could things really change so dramatically? Well, of course they could – but for *her* mum and dad? In two years' time, might she be talking about Mum's new boyfriend, Dad's new wife? Even about a baby half-brother or sister?

She rather wanted a brother or a sister. But not like *that*.

❦

After school, Nina found Aunt Rose adding the final flourishes to the shop window. The display area was draped in royal-blue curtains, and against this the White Lady wore navy trousers, a navy blouse and a navy jacket that would have made her blend into the background, had it not been for a flamboyant, wide-brimmed hat in traffic-stopping scarlet and a bead necklace that very nearly matched. Around the White Lady's feet, Aunt Rose had scattered various pieces of glass and china: willow-pattern plates, soap dishes, bowls and vases, and some long-stemmed artificial poppies that echoed the brightness of the hat and necklace. Really, as Aunt Rose's efforts went, it wasn't too bad.

After being interrogated about her day, saying hello to Jake in the cellar, and eating a slice of Aunt Rose's banana bread, Nina checked the displays and racks to see what new things had been put out.

She noticed something missing. 'Where's the crocodile?'

'Sold it this morning, dear,' said Aunt Rose.

'Who to?'

'I really can't remember, sweetheart. We've been busy today.'

Unaccountably disappointed, Nina went over to look at the books. The top shelves were crammed with romances, thrillers and crime – it was worrying, Aunt Nell joked, that Crowdenbridge people showed such relish for gory murders and multiple killings – with non-fiction on the wider shelves below. As Nina crouched to look, a word jumped out at her.

TOULOUSE.

Blue letters against a red and white background: *Plan de la Ville*.

She thought of the train ticket she'd carefully kept in the inside pocket of her rucksack – Toulouse to Paris, single. There had to be a link! She reached out for the thin book. As she opened it, a large sheet of paper unfolded itself, reaching down to her feet – it wasn't a book, but a map. Of course. *Plan de la Ville*. A street map.

'Hello, Nina. Found something you like?'

Nina turned. Sibyl was standing behind her, back braced, face almost hidden behind the armful of books she was carrying.

'Wait a minute.' Nina lifted three heavy ones from the top, and Sibyl struggled to put the rest down on a nearby stool.

Nina showed her the Toulouse map. 'Do you know how long this has been here?'

'Yes, dear,' said Sibyl. 'It came in on Friday.'

'Who brought it?' Nina's voice came out as a squeak.

'Usually I wouldn't know, but this time I do remember, because your aunts had popped out and I was in charge. She was a French lady and she asked if we'd take French books. Left another bag as well. We had a little chat. She works part-time at the boys' school in Hattersfield, apparently.'

Nina's heart was behaving like a yo-yo: leaping high, then plummeting at dizzying speed. 'Sir Frank Dalloway, you mean?'

'Yes, that's it. Nice lady.'

'Did you look in the other bag she left?'

'No, I just took the books. Left that to Beryl. She was sorting, that morning.'

Nina looked down at the map, reluctant to put it back. But it was meaningless now. She hadn't found a clue; instead she'd *lost* one. If the French lady had brought in the Toulouse map, then more than likely the jewelled evening bag had been hers, too, with the train ticket in it. Nothing to do with Mum at all. She felt hollow with disappointment.

At least she'd found out one useful thing: that the

black-and-silver cufflinks must belong to that French lady, *and* the photograph of the twins. Max might know her name, as she worked at his school.

Nina took out thirty pence to pay for the Toulouse map, without knowing quite why. As usual, Aunt Rose prodded and frowned at the till as if she'd never seen one before: stabbing at buttons, *Oh dear*-ing and *Silly me*-ing, and having to start all over again. At last the transaction was complete, Aunt Rose panting like someone who'd run hard for a bus.

When she'd recovered, Nina told her about the French lady.

'Oh, good,' said Aunt Rose, 'because I showed those cufflinks to Maurice – Mr Fotheringay, I mean ...' she was flustered, even blushing '... and he said they were very good quality. I mean, it's a pity he can't sell them for us, but better that we return them to their proper owner. If Max tells us her name, we'll make sure she gets them back.'

Jake came up from the cellar carrying a teddy bear. Without speaking, he handed it to Aunt Rose.

'Oh! How marvellous! Thank you, Jake.'

Jake nodded and went back down, while Aunt Rose and Nina examined the bear. Nina knew that old soft toys couldn't be sold in the shop, because they weren't marked with the toy safety symbol. But teddy bears could be valuable, especially old ones. This bear certainly was old, and well-cuddled, by the look of it – the fur was quite worn away on its head and tummy. In spite of its shabbiness, it had nice brown eyes, perky round ears and a smiley expression.

'Look, Nell, dear! What do you think of this?' Aunt Rose asked.

Aunt Nell, folding a duvet cover, scarcely gave the bear a glance. 'Throw it in the skip.'

'*Oh*, but—'

'I know you're always looking out for special bears, but this isn't one of them, I can tell you that much.'

'All the same,' said Aunt Rose, clutching it tightly, 'I think I might just show it to Maurice – Mr Fotheringay, I mean.'

'Oh, so we're on first-name terms now, are we?' said Aunt Nell. 'Go and show him then, if you don't mind wasting his time.'

Aunt Rose looked crestfallen for a moment, then bent down behind the counter, tucking the bear safely out of view. Then she bobbed up again to say, 'Oh, Nina! Ivy was in this morning, and I remembered to ask about your mum's boxes – and whether she could remember what was in them. She wasn't much help, sweetheart. The only thing she could remember is that elephant bag. The china seahorse was in it, and some sort of wrap cardigan, she said.'

That could be a small clue. If the wrap cardigan Mum wore for yoga had been inside, then certainly Mum hadn't meant the bag to come to the shop. Unless

– horrible thought – she was planning to give up yoga, give up her job with Tiffany, give up *everything*? Start a new life somewhere else, like Cat's dad had done?

Slowly, thoughtfully, Nina went down to the cellar, where she eyed the boxes and bags warily. There were so many of them. So much *stuff.*

Jake was there, with his radio on and a stack of boxes to sort through. Nina looked at him, wondering what it was like to have a breakdown. Once you'd had one, how could you be sure it wouldn't happen again?

She knew that Jake lived at Thrapston House, near the fire station. It was called sheltered accommodation, which meant that there was a warden in charge to make sure everyone was all right. Some of the children at junior school – when no grown-ups were listening – had called it *Crackpot House,* and used names like *weirdos* or *nutters* for the people who lived there. You'd see a group in the Co-op, with their attendants; they could be recognised by their shuffling movement, amazed expressions and effortful speech. Some, even though they were grown men or women, held tightly to the attendants' hands, like infants on an outing. The supermarket seemed to be strange and wondrous territory for them. Mum and the other checkout staff knew their names, and always had a chat and a joke with them.

Jake wasn't like that. He went out on his own. He had his volunteer work. Soon, Aunt Nell had told Nina, he'd be ready to look for a proper job.

'What's he *doing* there, at Thrapston House?' Nina asked. 'I mean, he's not – you know – like those other people there.'

Aunt Nell had said that it was a kind of rehabilitation, but that Jake was getting back on his feet, and would soon move out and find a flat on his own. Meanwhile, she said, helping in the shop seemed to be doing him good. He certainly looked quite happy now, sorting busily, singing occasional snatches of tunes.

Now that Toulouse and the evening bag had proved to be a dead end, Nina's thoughts returned to Max's monastery idea. Better to hold on to that, rather than admit she'd found out nothing whatsoever.

'Do you know a place called Lumberforth?' she asked Jake, who was shaking out what looked like thermal underwear.

'Llamas?' Jake said eagerly.

'*Llamas?*'

'Oh, nothing.' He looked embarrassed. 'Monastery, you mean?'

'Yes, that's it. Have you been there?'

'Know where it is. Why?'

'We need to get there,' Nina told him. 'Me and Max.'

'You'd need a car. S'out on the moors. No buses go that way.'

'P'raps we could walk.' Absent-mindedly, Nina started on a box of baby clothes and toys.

'Long way to walk,' Jake said. 'Miles.'

106

'We'll have to get a taxi, then.' Nina was thinking aloud. 'But I bet that would cost a lot, both ways. We'd never afford it, not without saving up for weeks. And we need to go *soon.*'

'Get a lift? Your aunts? Uncle?'

No, Nina definitely wasn't going to ask the aunts. She couldn't forget what they'd said about Mum. She wanted to prove that they'd got it all wrong.

'It's just that ...' Nina decided she could trust Jake. 'We think Mum might be there. On a retreat. We could get Max's mum or dad to drive us, only we don't want to tell anyone. We want to do it by ourselves. Please don't say anything to my aunts, will you?'

'I can drive,' said Jake, looking at her.

'*You* can?' Nina stared back, then realised how rude that might sound. 'I mean – I didn't realise you ever drove. You always walk everywhere.'

'Yeah. Passed my test. Two years ago. Before my breakdrown. I could drive you there and back.'

'*Would* you? Oh, Jake, that'd be brilliant!'

'Only I haven't got a car.'

'Oh.' Again, the flumping of spirits down to her ankles. It was exhausting, all this upping and downing. Of *course* Jake hadn't got a car. She knew that.

'Could borrow one, though. Pete, house manager, might lend me his van.'

'*Would* he?' Nina said, brightening again.

'I'll ask tonight. Tell you tomorrow.'

'Oh, thank you!' From the box in front of her, Nina took out a pink plastic pig that smiled at her encouragingly. 'Jake?' she ventured. 'Just now – you said break*drown*. Is that what you meant to say?'

'S'what I call it. What it was like.' Jake ripped parcel-tape off a box. 'Holding me down. Holding me under. Hard to breathe, let alone move.'

'Must have been *horrible.*' Nina tried to imagine. 'But – you're all right now, aren't you?'

'Yeah.' He lifted his head and shook it hard, like Zebedee shaking water from his ears, then smiled at her. 'I'll be OK.'

11

The Jade Buddha

———◆———

'I'm in Brighton,' said Dad, on the phone. 'When I told Clare, she remembered that Mum worked in a shop there for a while, before I knew her. A sort of hippy clothes shop called Indigo Moon. Kaftans, bangles, incense, that sort of shop. That's where I'm going – to see if I can find it.'

Nina wished him good luck, though she felt sure this must be a dead end. So Mum had lived in Brighton for a while? That didn't mean she was there *now*. Nina even felt a little smug, because Dad was uncovering Mum's past, while she and Max were interested in the present. Max's monastery idea had seemed unlikely at first, but what if he were right? Dad would feel a bit silly when he came back from his tour of long-ago friends and places only to find that Mum was a few miles up the road.

It seemed pointless, now, trying to phone Mum; Nina had given up expecting an answer. All she'd had, in response to her many text messages, was one saying, **Love you lots. Mum xxx** Not a word about coming home soon, or ever. But the plan of action was making Nina feel better. Purposeful.

She phoned Max about the French lady who taught at his school; he didn't know her, but said he'd investigate. Then, next afternoon, Nina sent an excited message saying that Jake was borrowing Pete's van on Wednesday, and would drive them to Lumberforth after school.

How to manage it, though – that was the next puzzle. Nina didn't want to tell the aunts. What if they said no, which she thought quite likely? They'd think it was a mad idea, and might not let her go off with Jake in a borrowed van. And Max's parents didn't know Jake, so – laid-back though they were – might not be keen on Max driving out to the moors with a stranger. She texted Max, who phoned back swiftly with a plan. Nina was to ask the aunts if she could go home with him after school. Max would tell his parents that he and Nina were going out with Zebedee. Jake could pick them up round the corner, by the church hall.

'See? Easy,' Max said happily. 'None of that's a *lie*.'

❦

At the fashion-show meeting on Wednesday, Nina and Cat were the only Year Sevens present; the rest were Sixth Form girls, and a couple of boys, and a few Year Tens and Elevens. Thea introduced Nina as a new helper, and everyone looked at her. It was at times like this that she was aware of how small she was, especially next to tall, willowy Cat.

'Oh, wouldn't it be lovely to be in the Sixth Form, and not have to wear uniform?' Cat sighed. Most of the people involved in the fashion show were studying art, like Thea, and dressing in an interesting way was clearly part of being an art student. There was a lot of black and fringing, fishnet tights and biker boots, but others preferred to steer away from Goth and develop their own style. Today, Thea was wearing a velvet jacket, customised with mismatched buttons and elbow patches, over skinny jeans; the cherry-red of the jacket clashed fabulously with her hair.

'She's a weirdo, your sister,' Tash had said to Cat, earlier, when Thea passed them in the corridor. But she couldn't quite disguise the admiration in her voice.

Preeyul, the girl in charge of advertising, produced a sheaf of posters. 'The Upcycling Fashion Show! Ta-daa!' She held one up. 'See, in case people expect bikes and Lycra, this shows what Upcycling is.'

The picture showed a pile of raggedy garments in a heap; a hand reached in to pull something out; a brighter drawing showed a bold-looking girl, quirkily and artistically dressed.

There was a buzz of excitement, as people threw in ideas for publicity: Facebook and Twitter; the local paper and radio; ticket-sellers round the school, at break and lunchtimes, dressed in fabulous clothes. Thea ran through the programme, another art student showed designs for the stage set, and a boy called Billy, who was to be DJ, played a selection of the music he'd chosen to create different moods.

'Look!' Nina's eyes were riveted to the outfits Thea had fastened to a big notice board. She'd pinned up the clothes in various poses to suggest arms and legs and bodies inside them. Nina was looking at a long, skinny indigo dress with tight sleeves, perfectly plain, apart from a rosette pinned to one shoulder – one of Mum's rosettes, the one she'd last seen on Cat's pencil case, the one made of scraps of clothes that had belonged to Mum, Dad and Nina. Scraps of their lives, tightly bunched, perfect together.

Nina held her breath. She couldn't help seeing it as a sign, a promise.

That morning, she'd picked up the jade-green Buddha and put him into her blazer pocket, wanting to take him with her to Lumberforth as a good-luck charm. She dipped her hand in to check that he was still there, and her fingers slid round the coolness of stone.

It felt like a good day, a day when things would go right.

❦

After school, on the bus, Nina could hardly sit still for excitement. She stayed on for a stop farther than usual, waiting for the one nearest Max's house.

'Aren't you getting off?' Cat asked, at the market square.

'I'm going to Max's,' Nina said, but because Cat deserved more, added, 'Tell you all about it tomorrow.'

Half an hour later, she, Max and Zebedee were waiting outside the church hall, and soon Jake pulled up in a white van. There was only one passenger seat, so Max climbed in at the back with Zebedee, squeezing in alongside a toolkit and some crates of electrical stuff.

'Jake, thanks for doing this,' said Max.

Jake gave an embarrassed shrug, and turned round to stroke, almost hug, Zebedee, who licked his face. Lots of people didn't like that, and Zebedee was always being told not to do it; Jake, though, seemed pleased.

Max had brought a map, but Jake knew the way without it. Driving carefully, he turned off the main road to Hattersfield, through a village and up a narrow lane, dry-stone-walled each side, that led to the high moors. Zebedee began to look out eagerly, expecting a walk.

The abbey came into view long before they reached it – a cluster of stone buildings, almost a village. There was a big gateway, a jumble of roofs, and, soaring above, the tower and arches of the abbey church. A huge wooden cross rose above one of the outer walls. The place looked both welcoming and forbidding, set on its exposed hillside, open to the gusts of moorland wind.

On one side there was a huddle of trees that leaned one way, as if they'd given up bracing themselves against the gales. It made Nina think of castles and sieges, and, at the same time, of boarding schools she'd read about in stories.

'Will they let us in?' she asked doubtfully.

'Course,' said Max. 'Monasteries don't turn people away.'

The van crept up the drive and through the big wooden gates. WELCOME TO LUMBERFORTH ABBEY, a sign said. ORDER OF ST BENEDICT. VISITORS WELCOME.

'See.' Jake pointed. 'We're OK.'

He parked the car, and they got out into the quiet of the courtyard. Signs pointed to REFECTORY, ABBEY CHURCH, SHOP. Many small windows, all with shutters, looked down from ivy-covered walls.

'There's a shop?' Nina said, surprised.

'Postcards and stuff,' said Jake. 'Prayer books.'

No one was around. They all stood self-consciously by the van. Even Zebedee waited quietly, not pulling on his lead. Nina slipped her hand into her pocket and closed her hand around the Buddha, feeling the smooth stone against her palm.

'Perhaps they're all at prayers,' Max suggested. 'Let's walk around a bit. I don't suppose anyone'll mind.'

Nina was already doubtful. Could Mum possibly be

behind one of those shuttered windows? Would she see them and come down?

'Let's try round here.' Max had turned a corner and found a path leading through a small stone arch. Jake and Nina followed, into a large walled garden, where two men were working: digging up potatoes, forking them into a wheelbarrow. They were monks, in long black robes, like dressing-gowns – not very practical, Nina thought, for gardening.

One of the monks saw them, and came over, smiling, dusting off his hands.

'Welcome to Lumberforth.' He didn't sound in the least surprised to see them.

What surprised Nina, though, was that this man was quite young – in his twenties, she thought, hardly older than Jake – and rather good-looking. She had expected monks to be grey-haired, stooped with age, and to have lived here for so long that they didn't know any other way of life, but this one looked more like a PE teacher. She noticed, poking out beneath the hem of his black robes, sturdy brown walking boots. Did he have trousers on as well, she wondered, or just pants? Then she quickly blinked the thought away, because it didn't seem polite to be thinking that about someone who was smiling pleasantly at her.

'Can I help you?' he prompted.

Since no one else seemed about to speak, Nina did. 'I'm sorry to bother you.' Her right hand was gripping the Buddha in her pocket. 'We're looking for someone. Her name's Miranda Flyte. We think she might be here, you know, staying for a while, on a ...' She'd forgotten the word.

'Retreat,' Max supplied.

'Oh.' The young monk looked a little perplexed. 'No, I don't think so. We do have retreats, four times a year, but the next one's not till October. There are no guests here at present.'

'She hasn't been here? You haven't seen her?' Nina asked.

'I haven't, but we do have quite a number of casual visitors. You could try at reception – over on the far side of the courtyard. Father Anthony will be able to help you. Lovely dog,' he added, bending to stroke Zebedee.

Nina and Max both thanked him, and he went back to his digging. Max didn't look at her as they crossed the courtyard. The crunch of their feet on gravel seemed to echo off the walls. Through the archway, the moorland scenery stretched far into hazy blue distance. This seemed a place quite apart from the ordinary world – remote from cars and shops and busyness.

And Mum wasn't here. Why had they ever thought she would be?

In reception – a small office all panelled in wood – a much older monk sat at a laptop computer. He looked eager to help, but shook his head slowly when Nina explained.

'No, I'm sorry.' He checked on his laptop. 'We haven't had a guest of that name. Let me check the October guest-list ... No, I'm afraid not. Sorry you've had a wasted journey. Let me give you this, just in case it's of any use. It's our programme of retreats and visitors' days.'

Nina and the others trailed back to the van. Zebedee looked expectantly at Max, still hoping for a proper walk, but then sensed the downcast mood and climbed in, tail low.

So much for Max's brilliant theory! Nina was annoyed with herself, now, for taking it so seriously. She'd thought it was crazy at first, but had let herself be drawn in, just because it had been better to have a mad idea than no idea at all.

'Er, sorry, Neen,' Max said, as Jake reversed. 'Sorry, Jake.'

Jake just shrugged, and said, 'No prob.'

'Waste of petrol.' Nina thought of Dad complaining about the prices, and how they were always going up. Although she had no idea how much petrol might cost, or how much this trip might have used, she added, 'We ought to pay you for it, Jake.'

'Nah.' Jake shook his head vigorously. 'Nice place, that.'

As the van pulled away, Nina looked back at the

cluster of buildings, the tower of the abbey church. She wondered what it was like to live there, and almost said so, but the weight of disappointment was too heavy. She took the Buddha out of her pocket and gave him a reproachful look. A lot of use *he'd* been!

Max was looking at the leaflet. 'Prayer and Mindfulness. Art and Spirituality. Tai Chi and Christian Meditation. Course, your mum might have used a different name. What d'you think she—'

'But she's not here *now*, is she?' Nina said sharply. 'And she most likely never has been. We might as well forget about it.' Her thoughts were returning to Brighton; she could only hope that Dad was on to something, after all.

'I liked Father Anthony with his laptop.' Max was quick to recover. 'I don't suppose they sit for hours copying out medieval manuscripts, not these days.'

Nina was thinking about the gardening monk. 'That first one we met – why would a young guy like that want to live in a monastery?'

'I wouldn't mind,' said Jake. 'Lovely up here. The moors and all.'

'You're kidding!' Max made a *pfff*ing sound. '*I'd* mind. I'd hate it. I mean, it's OK for a visit. But just imagine being stuck there, away from everything – no TV, no sport, no shops, no one to hang out with apart from old men. You can't tell me you'd put up with that if you didn't have to!'

'You'd have to do all the praying and stuff,' Nina said to Jake. 'To be a proper monk. You couldn't come and live here just because you like the moors.'

Max looked at her with a *duh* expression. 'Well, course!'

Jake said nothing, concentrating on steering round a series of twisty bends, pulling over to let a Land Rover pass.

'This isn't the way we came, is it?' Nina asked.

'No,' said Jake. 'There's this place I know. Not far. Want to call in. OK? Won't take long.'

'What sort of place?'

'Like a farm.'

'D'you know the name?' Max was unfolding his map.

'Yeah, it's ... here we are.'

The single-track lane swooped down into a dip. There on the bend was a collection of farm buildings, and a large stone house. Jake pulled in at the entrance, and Nina read, on a sign-board, LUMBERFORTH LLAMAS.

'Llamas! Here!' she exclaimed.

'Yeah. I've been before. Three or four times.' Jake was hurrying now, parking the van next to a Land Rover with a llama logo on the side; he jumped out, and went round to the back to open the doors for Max and Zebedee.

A young woman in jeans and a red fleece top was coming to meet them, smiling.

'Jake! What a lovely surprise!'

119

Jake grinned back, then shuffled his feet. 'Umm. Friends. Nina. Max. Zeb, the, um, dog. Just passing. Thought I'd say Hi.'

'You're very welcome.' The young woman included all of them in her smile. 'Come and see the llamas.'

12

The Green Crocodile

———•◦•———

It had turned out to be a very strange expedition: monks and llamas all in one afternoon. Nina was thinking about it in Mrs Fisher's Maths lesson: how surprising Jake was, how secretive! She hadn't known he loved animals so much, though she might have guessed from the way he'd greeted Zebedee.

Lumberforth Llamas was a llama trekking centre. Nina had never heard of such a thing, but it turned out that Jake had visited the farm, at first with a group, later on his own, as part of his rehabilitation after his breakdrown. That was how he knew Julie, the young woman in charge. She'd told them lots about llamas, and how being with them was good for people. You couldn't ride them, but a llama would carry your rucksack and walk steadily next to you while you held its halter-rope. At Lumberforth Llamas you could go on a llama trek, a llama picnic or even an overnight camping trek.

Having met several llamas in their stables, Nina thought she might like to try llama trekking for herself.

They were so gentle, with their enormous melting eyes, long-lashed, that gave them a bashful look. Their faces were camelly, only not as haughty as camels. Heads swayed on long necks as they gazed at her, nostrils flaring thoughtfully. Their legs were rather spindly for such big woolly bodies. When she stroked them their fur felt deep and soft and warm, and they made nice little humming or mooing sounds to each other. Yes, it would be easy to love llamas. One of them had leaned its head on Jake's shoulder to have its ears stroked, while he hummed to it softly. Another, in a separate stable, had a fluffy-coated baby lying beside her in deep straw. A baby llama was called a *cria*, Jake said.

'You don't know someone called Miranda Flyte, do you?' Nina asked Julie. Llama trekking and Mum – yes, that would fit. But Julie said that she didn't know the name.

Jake had promised to return Pete's van by six, so they couldn't stay long.

'Bye, Jake! Come and see us again soon!' Julie called, as they left.

'I will,' Jake told her. 'Soon as I've saved enough for a bike.' And he hummed happily to himself all the way back along the lanes.

❧

In Maths the next day, Nina's thoughts were wandering far away from fractions and percentages. She felt newly interested in Jake. He'd been really helpful yesterday, and had seemed to enjoy the outing more than anyone. And he kept surprising her, partly because he rarely said anything about himself, so finding out about him was a bit like searching through the bags in the shop, finding occasional treasures.

She did worry that he might break down again. What if he did? It sounded so dramatic. Nina imagined him crumpled by the roadside, wooden and lifeless as a puppet without strings. A rescue lorry would come for him; he'd be craned aboard and taken away to be mended.

He *looked* quite mended, especially when he smiled. And especially when he'd been with the llamas. You wouldn't have thought there was anything broken-down about him. It was only sometimes, when Nina glimpsed the frightened child inside, that she began to understand what Aunt Nell had told her about Jake needing time to recover.

Once – unforgettably – she had seen Jake crying. Down in the cellar, he'd taken something out of a box – a notebook with a pattern of cats on the cover. The sight of it had turned him rigid: completely still, except that his whole face seemed to be brimming, about to release a great wave of emotion. Nina saw how he struggled to contain it and felt frozen too, caught in the moment.

'What's wrong?' she asked, dismayed.

'My mum,' Jake said with difficulty. 'Had an address book. Same as this.'

'Is it hers?'

Jake shook his head. 'No. No. This is no good for the shop. Full of writing.' He chucked it into the crate that served as a rubbish bin, half turned his back on Nina and reached into the box of books, lifting out a pile of battered paperbacks. But she saw a big tear run down his cheek, then another; he brushed them away with his sleeve, and carried on sorting.

Nina felt helpless. She wished she could do something to take away his unhappiness. But she couldn't think what to say, since he so obviously wanted to pretend nothing was the matter.

When she asked Aunt Rose about Jake's parents, Aunt Rose said that she didn't think he had any. Perhaps that had contributed to his breakdown.

Could *Mum* have broken down, Nina wondered now? Might that be the answer?

But a broken-down person, surely, wouldn't make plans, the way Mum had seemed to make plans. They'd simply crash in a heap, the way Nina pictured it, and be unable to move. They'd stay where they were ...

'Nina? Perhaps you could tell us?' Mrs Fisher's voice sliced into her daydream.

'Um ...' Nina was jolted into stupidity, her eyes blurring. Figures on the whiteboard jumbled themselves into nonsense.

'Twenty-two and a half per cent,' Cat whispered.

'Twenty-two and a half per cent!' Nina repeated brightly.

'Hmm. Thank you, Caitlin. And, Nina, how exactly do we get that answer? Would you like to explain?'

'Um ...'

'I thought so. Not the slightest idea. Do pay attention, unless you want to spend your lunch break going through all this again.'

Thankfully, Nina managed to keep her lunchtime free. She told Cat about yesterday, the monastery and the llamas. Cat was interested, if a little scathing about Max's now discredited theory, but had other ideas to pursue.

'What about Tiffany? You haven't actually spoken to her, have you?'

'No. Dad did, on the phone.'

'You ought to go and see her. She might know something. Might have *heard* something. I'll come with you, if you want, on the way home.'

Nina wasn't sure, but – as Cat said – there was nothing to lose. They got off the bus together and went to Tiffany's in Lower Street, a large, barn-like place converted from a warehouse, with one large and two smaller studios. Tiffany was in reception, talking on the phone.

'Can you do tomorrow? Great. That would save my life, it really would.' She rang off, and looked at Nina without surprise. 'That's good. I've just found a new yoga teacher. The stand-in one wasn't popular at all. People were refusing to come to his class.'

'New? You mean, new as in ...'

'We'll see how we get on. You still don't know when your mum's coming back?'

'No,' Nina admitted.

She remembered to introduce Cat. Tiffany nodded, her hands busy tidying the reception counter. Nina had met her a few times, and thought her too sleek and brisk to have anything to do with yoga or meditation: blonde hair scraped back fiercely, beauty-counter make-up, tight black clothes, slim, muscled body. She always seemed in a hurry, as she did now; she turned towards the back office, looking over her shoulder to ask, 'What can I do for you, then?'

'Um ... I just wondered if Mum had phoned, or anything ...' Nina's voice trailed off.

'No. Not a word. I do know that Stella gave her a lift to the station, the day she left. Stella told me this morning.'

'Stella?'

'She's in Miranda's yoga class. *Was.* Hated the stand-in teacher so much she's swapped to Thursday Pilates.'

'And she gave Mum a lift to the station?' Nina's thoughts were racing; she saw railway lines stretched out like spidery limbs across a map of England, carrying Mum away in all directions at once.

'Can we talk to Stella? Have you got her phone number?' Cat asked.

'She works at the florist's most afternoons.' Tiffany gestured with her head. 'You'll find her there.'

Out on the pavement, Nina and Cat looked at each other.

'So this Stella was the last person to see your mum! She must be able to tell us *something*.'

'Come on!' Nina felt giddy with excitement, forgetting to look before she crossed the road, and stepping into the path of a bike.

The cyclist swerved and shouted, and Cat dragged Nina back just in time. 'Getting yourself run over won't help.'

The florist's was round the corner in Chapel Street. Buckets of blooms spilled out on to the pavement in an extravagant floral wave, and the small space inside was heady with the mingled scents of lilies, roses and chrysanthemums. Nina looked hopefully at a plump, aproned woman who was snipping stems and bunching flowers into a sheaf.

'Excuse me – are you Stella?'

'No, love. Stella's off this afternoon. Hospital appointment. She'll be in tomorrow, usual time.'

Tomorrow. It seemed an unreachable age away. Nina sagged with disappointment.

'We'll try again then,' Cat promised, and set off to walk the mile home to Settlebank, across the river. Nina went to Second-Hand Rose, where she was met by Aunt Nell in stern mood.

'Nina? I think we need to have words.'

Oh, dear. This didn't sound good. Aunt Nell led her into the storeroom at the back, where no customers could hear.

'You told us you were going to Max's yesterday, didn't you? But one of our customers saw you and Max and his dog getting into a white van by St Mary's Church Hall. Was she right? Was that you?'

'Um. Yes.'

Aunt Nell's look sharpened. 'I think you'd better explain.'

'Well, you see ... it all turned out to be pointless, really ...'

There was nothing for it but to tell her about Max's idea, the hunt for Mum, his certainty that she was on a monastic retreat.

Aunt Nell looked puzzled. 'But why on earth didn't you say? And who took you there? Who was driving the van?'

Nina had carefully left this out. Her mouth opened. It wouldn't be fair to get Jake into trouble too, but what else could she say?

'Erm ... it was Jake.'

Aunt Nell's eyebrows shot up, wrinkling her forehead. '*Jake!* I didn't know he could drive.'

'Well, he can. It wasn't his fault. He offered. He

borrowed the van specially. As a favour. He wouldn't even let us pay for the petrol.'

'I see.' Aunt Nell gave a big sigh. 'At least you didn't go off with some complete stranger, which is what I'd imagined.' Her face softened. 'Nina, I know you're very worried about your mum. That's not surprising. But you must remember that we're in charge of you, Aunt Rose and I and Uncle Derek. We need to know where you are! Why didn't you tell the truth, instead of pretending you were at Max's?'

'Because you might not have let me go.' There seemed nothing for it but to be truthful.

Aunt Nell huffed. 'If you'd just *told* us about Max's idea, we could have phoned the monastery, and there'd have been no need for secrets and plotting. Don't do it again, please.'

'Sorry,' Nina mumbled.

But she couldn't be *really* sorry. The outing had been a waste of time in terms of finding Mum, but she'd seen the monastery and met some monks, learned a bit more about Jake and been introduced to llamas. She couldn't wish she hadn't gone.

'You remind me of your dad, when he was a little boy.' Aunt Nell was smiling now. 'When he was about nine, he and a friend had the idea of walking to John O'Groats. They went as far as Tiptonstall Woods, then got hungry and came home.'

It was odd to Nina to think of Dad as a little boy,

being looked after by his aunts. 'Was he naughty?'

'He had his moments. There was the time he refused to speak for two days because we wouldn't let him keep piranhas in the bath.' Aunt Nell opened the door into the shop. 'Let's get you a drink. And Aunt Rose has made fat rascals.'

Jake wasn't here today, but the green crocodile was; Aunt Rose showed her. 'See! It's like a homing-pigeon, that croc! Always finds its way back.'

The crocodile was lying smugly along a top shelf above the toys, as if it belonged there.

'What happened this time? Did it scare someone?'

'We don't know, dear. I found him in a bag of pillowcases.'

Nina was delighted. It felt like a good sign. The crocodile smiled at her with its double row of pointy teeth, reassuring her that things would soon get better.

❧

When Dad phoned that evening, after supper, Aunt Nell spoke to him first. There was a telephone table in the hallway, with a seat next to it, and a shelf for the directories, and a notepad and pen for messages; the phone was an old-fashioned one, the handset tethered to its base by a spirally flex. Phone conversations could be overheard from almost anywhere in the house. So Nina wasn't exactly eavesdropping; she just waited at the top of the stairs to her room, knowing that Aunt Nell would call her in a minute.

'Now, Richard.' Aunt Nell was using her no-nonsense voice. 'I really think you ought to come back home. Nina needs you! No, it's not that we mind having her to stay, you know that. She's no trouble at all – in fact she's been helping nearly every day in the shop. Mmm … mmm … yes. But it's unsettling for her, not being in her own home. And never knowing where you'll be off to next. Mmm … mmm … no, I see. But where's all this getting you? To say nothing of the *work* you must be losing. Oh, really? Well. If you say so. Yes, you'd better tell her yourself. Bye then. Good luck, dear – and take care. NINA!' she shouted. 'Here's Dad on the phone!'

Nina had expected Aunt Nell to tell Dad about yesterday's deception, but she hadn't, and Nina was grateful for that.

'Nina,' Dad said, when he'd been through the usual Dad-questions, 'I'm going to be … well, the thing is, I'm going to be away for a bit longer than I thought – until the weekend, at least.'

'Oh. Where are you? Still in Brighton?'

'Yes. I might be on to something. Trust me, precious.'

'But why can't you *tell* me?' Nina burst out. 'You're as bad as Mum, making a great mystery out of it!'

'I don't want to get your hopes up for nothing. Nina, you're being brilliant about all this. Just wait another day or so.'

'Another day or so? How *many* days?' Nina humphed. 'And I'm not being brilliant. I'm just being *me*.'

'That's exactly what I mean. Being your brilliant self. Just hold on a bit longer, sweetheart.'

And no matter how Nina pleaded, she could get no more out of him.

'Well, Nina,' Aunt Nell said brightly, when Nina trailed down to the kitchen for no particular reason, 'I think we'd better call round at home to collect a few more of your things. Your walking boots, you wanted? And maybe a few more clothes, or books.'

'Yes, please. When?' Nina said, a new idea forming.

'Let's see. Tomorrow, straight after school?'

Aunt Rose was busy making coffee. 'Have you forgotten it's Friday tomorrow? The man's coming for the electrical tests at four. You need to be there for that. Shall I go with Nina?'

'Oh, yes. If you don't mind, dear,' said Aunt Nell.

Good! Aunt Rose would be far easier to distract than Aunt Nell. Nina was already imagining herself in Mum and Dad's bedroom, fetching a chair to climb up to the shelf-space above their wardrobe, where Mum kept old photograph albums from the days before all the photos were stored on the computer. And now Nina was trying to work out what Dad was up to, as well as Mum. There must be something that would tell her.

She went upstairs to send a text message to Max.

13

The Elephant Bag

———◆———

Waking up, Nina gazed around her attic bedroom. From below came the soft, rhythmic sound of Uncle Derek snoring; the house was in darkness, apart from the small glow from a night light on the landing.

Her mind was muzzy with sleep, afloat on the remnant of a dream. She reached out to turn on the lamp, then lay down, puzzling. All she knew was that she badly wanted to return to that dream, without quite remembering what it had been.

If she let her thoughts drift ...

She closed her eyes, turned over and curled herself up. Her mind drifted pleasantly. She was sitting on a cushiony sofa, next to her big panda. Her legs, in stripy socks, stuck out in front of her, much too short to reach the floor, and the television was on, with Christmas-tree lights reflected in its screen. A babysitter was doing something in the kitchen, and Mum and Dad were ready to go to a New Year's Eve party. A smart one, it must be, because Dad wore a jacket and bow tie, and Mum was all in black too, with glittery black earrings and her hair caught up into a black flower pin. When Mum bent down for a goodbye kiss, Nina smelled perfume – not the patchouli Mum usually wore, but something more grown-up, as if she were pretending to be an elegant, glamorous person, used to smart parties. As she leaned forwards, the small bag she wore over her shoulder swung on its silk cord – an evening bag, palest, delicate blue, spangled with tiny glass beads that caught the colours of the Christmas-tree lights. Nina reached out to touch it, feeling the graininess of seed pearls against fine fabric.

'You look lovely, Mum!' she murmured, wishing she could go too.

'Thank you, poppet! You be good. We'll see you in the morning. It'll be next year!'

Dad kissed her too, and Nina giggled and said, 'See you next year' and woke up.

She lay staring into the darkness.

Had she been dreaming? Or remembering?

The bag! The beaded evening bag!

Was her mind playing tricks, making a memory out of something she wanted to believe was true? Or was that really Mum's bag that had been returned to the shop, as her instinct had told her when she saw it?

She closed her eyes and lived the dream again. It began to seem stiff and rehearsed, not real at all; doll-figures dressed up, not Mum and Dad. And now it was Friday, and time to get up.

Mum's latest text was exactly the same as the one before.

Love you lots. Mum xxx

It might have *been* the old one, re-sent. Maybe Mum couldn't even be bothered to key in a new message. Nina texted back, **You said that last time. What does it mean?** She was rather pleased with this hint at reproach and exasperation, while sticking to the simple fact. Maybc it would goad Mum into sending something new.

Nina was in the Science lab, supposedly heating copper sulphate crystals with a Bunsen burner, when she heard the trickle of notes for an incoming message. It was impossible not to look.

The message wasn't from Mum, but from Max.

Spk Mme hv nws fon L8r

Nina puzzled over this for a few moments before deciding that Max had spoken to the French lady who taught at his school, and would phone with news later. Unfortunately, Mr Bell, the Science teacher, had crept up behind her, with the result that her mobile phone was confiscated and locked up in his desk.

'You can collect it at the end of school,' he told her.

'But—'

'You're aware of the school rules, I think? Mobile phones are to be switched off during lessons.'

'Sir, you're not allowed to take people's personal

property!' That was Tash, either sticking up for Nina (unlikely, Nina thought) or making a point of principle. 'That's well out of order.'

'I don't need advice from you either, young lady. Rules are rules.'

Today hadn't got off to a very good start. In the next lesson, French, Nina couldn't find her favourite gel pen, the one that wrote so nicely and smoothly. She hadn't zipped up her pencil case and everything had fallen out into the elephant bag, but when she groped around for the missing pens and pencils she could only find half of them.

Then her reaching fingers met with a fringe of frayed lining, right at the bottom. The elephant bag was lined with a satiny fabric that had worn into a hole. The missing pens had slid through into the space between the lining and the thicker fabric of the outer bag.

Nina had to work the hole a bit bigger to get her fingers through and find the pens, all the while trying to attend to the conjugation of *être* and *avoir*. With her fingertips she felt something else in there, too – a folded piece of paper. Carefully she eased it out and unfolded it.

Mum's writing! In flamboyant purple. A name, and an email address:

Pascal Gaultier, pg@beauregard.fr

An email address. A name, a French name. Why did everything seem to point towards France?

It was another Clue! Perhaps an important one. But how long had the slip of paper been there? It might have been *years*.

At break, Nina showed Cat, who said at once, 'Pascal Gaultier! That's your mum's new man, I bet. French! Nice name.'

At once Nina hated it. She hated *him*. She could see him: smarmily handsome, in an old-fashioned film-star sort of way. He'd have perfect manners, and smoke French cigarettes that made a romantic blue haze. She was certain he'd flattered and oozed his way into Mum's life with the aim of luring her away.

'There's one way to find out,' Cat said. 'Email him and ask.'

'What, just like that? *Have you stolen my mum? Are you her new man?*'

Cat nodded.

'The problem is, how? Uncle Derek and the aunts have got email. But it'd be really hard to send a message and get one back without them knowing.'

'We can email from the library,' Cat said. 'We'll do it at lunchtime. Course, Pascal Gaultier could be the name of a shop, or just someone she met, not her man at all.'

'But we can't not try to find out.'

In the library, Cat had the idea of using her own email address rather than Nina's. 'Then you needn't worry about using your aunts' computer, and if he replies today I can text you straight away.'

Together, with many drafts and deletions, they composed a message: *Dear Monsieur Gaultier, I am Nina, the daughter of Miranda Flyte, and I think you might know where she is. If you do, could you please email back? I am very worried about my mother. Thank you very much, Nina Flyte (via Caitlin Eagleton, friend)*

Nina clicked *Send.* 'Now we wait. And hope he's not one of those people who only check their emails once a week.'

❧

At the end of school, retrieving her mobile phone, Nina almost missed the bus, because the science block was at the opposite end of school from the bus bay. She ran till she thought her lungs would burst, and hauled herself aboard, panting, just as the driver was about to close the doors.

Cat was sitting next to Thea, but had saved Nina a seat behind them. She flopped into it, and listened to a voicemail message from Max: 'Where are you? Why isn't your phone on? Call me when you can.'

Nina tried, but now Max wasn't answering. He'd be on his way back from Hattersfield on the train; there wasn't always a signal for mobiles. 'It's me. I'll try later,' she told voicemail, and put the phone away.

Cat and Thea, in the seat in front, were talking about the fashion show, and the items they still needed.

Thea turned round to include Nina in the conversation. 'Tomorrow, we're going to put all the outfits together. Accessories and everything. Would you like to come round and help?'

'Yes, please!' It would make a nice change from all this *worry*.

'We'll meet you in the shop, then. We're still looking for a few bits and pieces. About eleven?'

'We'll tell Mum. You can stay for lunch,' added Cat. 'And we're going to the flower shop now, aren't we?'

'The flower shop?' said Thea, but Cat only tapped her nose. 'It's a secret.'

At the market square, they both waved to Thea as the bus pulled away. Stella *had* to be at the florist's today!

'What if her hospital thing was serious, and they've kept her in?' Nina puffed, as they sprint-walked along Chapel Street. But there was a different person in the florist's today, sitting at the counter, writing in a book. Not the plump aproned lady of yesterday – this one had to be Stella. Mummish sort of age, she had a bouncy fringe, dangly earrings and hair in a high ponytail. As the two girls entered she raised her head and stared.

'Oh!' she said, before Nina could speak. 'Your bag!'

'This?' Nina had the elephant bag over her shoulder, stuffed with weekend homework. School bags were supposed to be plain-coloured, as her Year Head had mentioned more than once; in fact Nina had a new black rucksack bought specially, but wanted to keep Mum's special bag with her all the time.

'It's just that my yoga teacher had one just like that,' said the woman-who-must-be-Stella.

'You mean Miranda,' said Nina, 'Miranda Flyte?'

'Yes! Do you know her?'

'She's my mum. I'm Nina and this is Cat.'

Stella looked relieved. 'Oh, good! She found it, then.'

'Found it?'

'I'm so glad. She seemed quite upset. So you're Nina? You're very like her! She's such a lovely teacher, your mum – I've been in her class since Christmas. Anyway, did she have a good holiday?'

Holiday?

'Actually, she's not quite back yet.' Nina was wondering how she could find out everything Stella knew without revealing that she knew nothing herself, but it was Cat who said, 'About the bag. Had Nina's mum lost it, then, when you took her to the station that day?'

'Yes. She was in quite a bother. That's what made her late for the train. After the class, she told us she was going away for a couple of weeks, and we all wished her a nice time – then she went off, and a few of us had coffee together, as we usually do. I'd taken the afternoon off to go shopping in Hattersfield, and as I set off in the car I saw your mum again, Nina, with a big case on wheels. She seemed in such a hurry, I pulled over to see if she wanted a lift. She was anxious about missing her

140

train, so I suggested taking her to Hattersfield, because the fast trains stop there but not here. She could get whichever train came first for London – the Leeds one, or the other way to Manchester.'

'London?' Cat prompted.

Stella nodded. 'So it's a city break, is it? Nice, and she's had time to do lots of things while she's there. Is she staying with friends? I expect you're looking forward to having her back.' It was lucky that Stella wasn't the sort of conversationalist who waited for answers.

'Did she say anything about Brighton?' Nina tried.

'I don't think so. Only London, St Pancras. If she was going *on* to Brighton, she didn't say anything about it.'

'And what did she say about the elephant bag?' Nina waggled the strap.

'Oh, she'll be so pleased you found it! She usually takes that bag to the studio, but she hadn't been able to find it that morning. So she thought she must have left it in the changing room, the week before. It wasn't there either, so she had another search at home, and that was what made her late. But you've got it now, so all's well. Did you find the seahorse, as well?'

'The seahorse?'

'Yes, she'd lost that, too. It was a present for Tiffany – to make up for going off on holiday so suddenly, she said, and leaving her in the lurch.'

'No, that's all right,' Nina said, glad of something she *did* know. 'I've got the seahorse. And the elephant bag.'

'Good. That's a mystery solved, then. Do say hello to your mum for me, and I must say I'll be *really* pleased when she's back. Whatever that man tried to make us do, it wasn't yoga the way we do it with your mum.'

Nina and Cat thanked Stella and left the shop, pausing outside the baker's window on the corner.

'So,' said Cat. 'What have we learned? That your mum left by train, for London. And she talked about a holiday.'

'And we know she didn't mean the elephant bag to go to the shop.' Nina hugged it to her side.

'Has your mum got friends in London?'

'No! None that I've heard of. Mum *hates* London. She doesn't like big cities. London's the *last* place she'd go for a holiday.'

14

The Jewelled Evening Purse

———◆———

Cat set off for home, saying that she'd check her emails as soon as she got in. Nina walked round to Second-Hand Rose, slightly dazed, needing to think about everything she'd just heard.

Aunt Rose was waiting by the till with her coat on. 'I thought we'd go straight away, sweetheart.'

Nina had forgotten all about going home to collect things. Somehow, the information from Stella and the link to Pascal Gaultier made the quest feel sharper and more urgent, as if Mum had just this minute left, scattering clues everywhere.

It felt strange to be walking down her own street with Aunt Rose; like returning from a long journey.

'You're very quiet, dear!' Aunt Rose remarked. 'Are you all right? Tired out after school, I expect. Your first full week.'

Nina was thinking about the name *St Pancras*. It made her think of yesterday's biology lesson: liver, pancreas, kidneys, heart and lungs, a diagram of a body with its front neatly sliced and hinged open like a lid. But it was St Pancras, not St Pancreas, and there was something lurking on the edge of her mind . . .

'Aunt Rose? If you wanted to go to Brighton, would you get a train from St Pancras?'

'Well, dear, I'm not sure, these days – it's all change. St Pancras is where you get the Eurostar train to Paris. I keep telling Nell we ought to make the effort and book ourselves a long weekend. All the way to Paris by train! It's hard to believe. I haven't been there since my honeymoon. Back then, we went by cross-Channel ferry.'

Eurostar.

Paris.

Pascal Gaultier.

It was all starting to add up to something Nina didn't like one bit. Had Mum gone to Paris with Pascal Gaultier – or gone to meet him there? And a horrible thought came into her mind. What if it were really Pascal Gaultier who'd sent the birthday lilies, and Mum had lied about them being from the Co-op girls? Would Mum lie like that?

Mum had always been good at French. Was that because she spoke French with Pascal Gaultier? And did that mean she'd known him for a long time?

Oh, it was too much, all this thinking and wondering and guessing! What Nina wanted was an *answer.* And she intended to find it here, at home.

At the front door, Aunt Rose found the key in her purse after much rummaging and muttering. They stepped inside, over a small heap of letters and catalogues on the doormat. Aunt Rose stooped to gather them up, and carried them through to the kitchen table.

Home. Nina stood sniffing, not sure what it smelled of, exactly, but she'd have known where she was if someone had led her in blindfolded. It wasn't furniture polish and air-freshener, like the aunts' house; the smell here was made up of comfortableness and welcome and familiarity. It felt cold, though. The house needed people in it, to breathe life and warmth. It needed *Mum*.

Aunt Rose picked a piece of fluff off the carpet. 'I think I'll just run round with the vacuum cleaner while I'm here. Might as well make myself useful. You've got your list, haven't you, dear? You get your things and we'll be done in a jiffy.'

Passing the phone, Nina thought of checking for messages. There were seven – one from Tiffany, one for Dad: 'Sorry, Richard, but you haven't returned my call and I've waited long enough. I've found someone else to do the work.'

That didn't sound good! The rest were from Angie, the Co-op manager. Nina listened to all of them:

'Miranda? Sorry to hear you can't come in today. We'll see you on Monday. Give me a call if you get the chance.'

145

'Miranda – I was expecting you at eight. Is there something wrong?'

'Miranda, I really need to know whether you'll be in tomorrow.'

'Miranda. Can you phone back, please, as soon as you receive this? If you're off sick you'll need a medical certificate.'

'Miranda. Please get in touch. Today. This really isn't good enough.'

Oh, dear. It didn't sound as if Mum could count on walking back into her job, when or if she came back. The final message had been left last Thursday – there was nothing since.

Upstairs on the landing, Nina texted a message to Mum: **Co-op left lots msgs**, and sent that. Then a second: **Got yr elephant bag! + aunts hve seahorse.** She waited for *Message Sent*, thinking of the oddness of messages flying about – where would Mum be when she read them? Where were the messages if *no one* read them? Did they float about like wisps of smoke, gradually fading?

Her own bedroom welcomed her, looking slightly sad and unused.

The phone trilled in her hand. Not Mum, but Max.

'Got you at last! Listen. I found out about that French lady.' Max was talking almost faster than Nina could think. 'She's not exactly a teacher – she comes in to do French conversation with the A-Level students.

146

Madame Lestrange, her name is. Well, today I saw her in the corridor, so I asked if she took the map of Toulouse to your aunts' shop, and she said yes she had. Then ...' Max paused for effect '... I asked if that beady purse thing was hers as well.'

'And?'

'*Non, non, I know nuzzing about any bag,*' Max said in an Inspector Clouseau accent. '*I donated ze map wiz some uzzair books and a pair of shoes – zat was all.* She doesn't really sound like that, but you get the idea. Then, of course, she wanted to know why I was asking, so I explained about the valuable cufflinks and the photo of twins. No, she said, nothing to do with her. Couldn't have been. She'd never been in your aunts' shop, till that day.'

Nina's dream came rushing back. Her heart thumped with certainty, and new, surging hope.

'Neen?' Max was saying. 'Course, it still doesn't mean the bag has anything to do with your mum—'

'But it *does*. It *is* hers. I know it is. Thanks, Max. I'll call you later, OK?'

Nina sat on the bed, her head whirling.

Mum. The photo. The cufflinks. The train ticket from Toulouse. Now St Pancras and Eurostar and Pascal Gaultier.

And there were the twins. Who were the twins?

It all *had* to mean something, if only she could see what.

Now she must make the most of her time here. It took only a few moments to collect her walking boots, and some extra T-shirts from a drawer. The vacuum cleaner was humming away downstairs; Aunt Rose's idea of a jiffy would surely turn out to be fifteen minutes or more, especially as neither Mum nor Dad was hot on hoovering, and it probably hadn't been done for some while. Nina sent a quick text message to Dad: **Think Mum's in France**. Then she tiptoed through to her parents' bedroom, feeling like a thief.

It only made sense if Pascal Gaultier was involved, and he'd enticed Mum to Paris ... it was a romantic thing that grown-ups liked to do. Not Mum and Dad; they were always too busy with everyday things like shopping and work and ironing. Grown-ups who were lovers, though – trips to Paris were just the sort of thing *they* did. Nina had seen adverts.

'But Mum! How *could* you?' Nina whispered. Were Mrs Enderby and spiteful Jem right after all?

Nina had brought Mum's Buddha with her and now replaced him on the bedside table, since he didn't seem to be doing much to help, but her main mission was to look in the top cupboard. There was a white chair with curly legs in the bedroom, that Mum sometimes sat on to dry her hair by the mirror. Nina pulled it over to the wardrobe, climbed on to it, and slid back the doors above the hanging-space. She'd never looked inside before, but she knew that Mum kept secret things there, like presents.

A memory surfaced in her mind – a memory from long ago, of Mum, unaware that Nina was watching, standing on this chair to reach to the very back. 'Mum?' Nina heard her own childish voice, and saw how Mum turned quickly, her face guilty – yes, guilty. She climbed down from the chair and started talking loudly; Nina couldn't remember what about, but it had been something unimportant, like what to have for tea.

Nina frowned with the effort of holding this in her mind, but it slithered out of reach, like a slippery fish. Like a dream.

She looked into the cupboard space. There was an old sun hat, and some knitting Mum had started but never finished. There was the old photograph album, a rolled-up sleeping bag, and a checked blanket used for summer picnics. Quickly she pulled out the album and flipped through its pages. Pictures of Mum and Dad together, relaxed and smiling, some of Mum on her own, then Mum holding a baby wrapped in a white shawl. *That's me!* Nina thought, with a jolt of disbelief. She turned the pages that showed her baby self: lying on a blanket, then sitting up, crawling, and taking first tottery steps, holding Dad's hands.

Twins, Nina was thinking. Twins. She remembered, without any effort at all, an afternoon in the aunts' shop – someone coming in with twin babies in a buggy, and Mum going to look. 'Twins – how lovely!' she'd said, bending close, and – Nina heard it clearly now – there was sadness in her voice. Sadness? For what?

Could *Mum* be a twin? Did that make any sense at all? But no – the photograph was of boys. Unless they were girls dressed to look like boys. Could one of them have been Mum? And where was that photo now? Still in the drawer at the shop, unless someone had thrown it away, which Nina fervently hoped hadn't happened. She would have another look at the first chance.

She flicked through all the album's pages, then pushed it to one side and reached farther back.

Right in the corner, almost beyond the reach of her arm, was a large maroon-coloured bag. Nina stood on tiptoes to stretch for it.

There was something soft inside, and something hard.

Nina stepped down from the chair. The bag, folded over on itself, was a large carrier, completely plain – no shop name to give a clue. Inside was something made of gauzy fabric. Nina pulled it out, and found herself looking at a skimpy dress – bodice covered in net, a narrow waist, skirts flaring, petal-shaped. Deep, deep red, a colour that would make Mum look mysterious and dramatic.

A dancer's dress. Well, it wasn't surprising that Mum had kept one of the costumes from her dancing days.

There was more. A pair of red shoes, well-worn and scuffed; not ballet pumps, but heeled shoes with buttoned bar fastenings. Shoes you could dance in.

And a programme. A folded leaflet.

Concours de Danse. Avignon, 15 mai, she read. And there was a lot of smaller print, all in French.

France again! It couldn't be a coincidence.

Nina decided to take the programme with her to read later, but now she'd better put everything back as it was. The vacuuming had stopped, and she'd lost all sense of how long she'd been here. She put the dress and the shoes back into the bag, and climbed on to the chair.

In her hurry she wasn't as careful as the first time. The chair was only a flimsy one. First it creaked as she adjusted her weight; then one of its legs gave way, and it lurched to one side. Nina's foot went right through the seat, with a horrible splintering. Next moment she was sprawling on the floor with the chair clamped painfully to her right leg.

Ouch! Before she had time to inspect the damage, Aunt Rose was pounding up the stairs.

'Nina, sweetheart! What was that crash? Are you all right?'

'I'm fine, thank you.' Nina tried to smile, though she could feel the trickle of blood down her ankle.

'What were you *doing*?'

'Just looking for something in the top of the wardrobe.'

Aunt Rose gave a squawk, seeing the blood. 'Your poor leg! Oh, dear, does it hurt? Does it need stitches? Let me see ...' Stiffly she knelt on the carpet.

With more wrenching and splintering, Nina prised herself free. 'It's only a little cut. But the chair ...'

The chair was in a bad way. One leg had come right off, and another splayed out at a strange angle; the seat had a big, jagged, foot-sized hole in it.

'You really shouldn't have stood on it, dear,' said Aunt Rose. 'But I expect it can be mended. I'm more worried about that cut, in case it's got splinters in it. Where do Mum and Dad keep first aid things?'

Nina thought there might be a box under the kitchen sink. She got to her feet, and tried standing and then walking. Not too bad.

At last the cut was examined, washed and plastered, and Aunt Rose had satisfied herself that they needn't call an ambulance, and that Nina might well survive without a blood transfusion. 'Can you face walking back, sweetheart? Or should I get Uncle Derek to fetch us in the car?'

Nina assured her that she could walk. Aunt Rose was so busy treating her as the lucky survivor of a mountaineering accident that she didn't think to ask what Nina had been looking for. As soon as they arrived back at the shop, though, Aunt Nell got straight to the point.

'What were you doing that meant clambering on a chair?'

'I was looking for clues. I found this. And some old dancing clothes of Mum's.' Nina produced the dance programme from her rucksack.

Both aunts studied it.

'It's a clue,' Nina said. 'I thought— I think Mum's gone to France.'

They both looked at her: Aunt Rose sadly, Aunt Nell with an enquiring expression.

'What makes you think that, dear? This must be years old.' Aunt Nell picked up the programme and held it close to her nose, finding a date. 'Yes. This was sixteen years ago. Before your mum and dad had even met!' She gave Nina one of her rare hugs. 'I know you're desperate to find something out, Nina dear, but you're only going to be disappointed if you—'

Ting! went the door. In came a young woman in a flowered raincoat, carrying a box. Her face was sad and radiant, both at the same time.

'This was my dad's.' She put the box down on the counter. 'He wanted you to have it. It's worth quite a lot.'

15

The Marble Chess Set

————◆•◆————

'Oh, has your father passed away?' said Aunt Rose. 'I'm so sorry.'

The young woman looked as if she'd done all the crying she was going to do, and was now smiling bravely. 'Yes. Thank you. He was at the Cottage Hospital, you see, for quite some while, so he wanted to donate his chess set to your shop. It was his prized possession.'

'That's very kind,' said Aunt Nell. Both aunts were looking into the box, and Nina edged closer, too.

'See, it's beautiful.' The young woman lifted out the board, chequered in clouded white and sea-green, then took out two pieces, one of each colour. 'Marble. Hand-carved. My father did a lot of travelling, and he bought this in China, from the craftsman who made it. There's so much character in the faces – look. Even all the pawns are different. See the detail?'

'Gorgeous!' said Aunt Rose.

'Quite astonishing,' agreed Aunt Nell.

The young woman turned the board over to show

small Chinese letters engraved in one corner. 'This is the signature of the master craftsman. He lives in a remote mountain village in north-west China, and he makes one chess set every five years, because that's how long it takes. There are only six of his chess sets in the whole world, each in a different style. All the others are still in China.'

Aunt Rose seemed lost for words, but Aunt Nell said, 'Remarkable! And you're quite sure you want to give it to us? You don't want to keep it, in memory of your father?'

The young woman shook her head. 'It *is* lovely, but he made it quite clear that he wanted it to raise funds for the hospital. It's written in his will.'

'We know just the person to help us. Don't we, dear?' Aunt Nell looked at Aunt Rose, who smiled and nodded. 'Our very good friend deals in antiques, and he's especially interested in chess sets. This is far too valuable to sell here in the shop, but Mr Fotheringay could sell it for us, getting the best price. Would your father approve of that?'

The woman said that he most certainly would. Aunt Nell wrote down her name, address and phone number, promised to let her know what happened, and put the chess pieces back in the box.

'Rose,' said Aunt Nell, when the woman had gone, 'I think Mr Fotheringay should see this at once, don't you?'

'Ooh, yes,' agreed Aunt Rose. 'Shall we all go? This is so exciting!'

'Yes. Sibyl can look after the shop for a few minutes.'

'Is Jake here?' Nina asked. It would be closing time soon, and she hadn't even put her head round the cellar door to say hello.

'No, dear. He had to go off somewhere,' Aunt Rose told her.

'But Jake never goes anywhere!'

'Well, today he has. Do be quick, please, Nell, dear. I don't want to miss Maurice. He sometimes locks up early on Fridays.'

Nina noticed that Aunt Rose was smoothing her hair back, and making little dabs at her cheeks, as they hurried along the street.

Nina pulled out her mobile phone, wondering if Dad had replied. Instead there was a text from Max: **NEthng nu?**

And just at that moment the trickle of notes announced a new message: Dad.

How did you know? On way to Le Havre. Will phone later.

The aunts had gone ahead into the antiques shop; through the window, Nina saw Mr Fotheringay getting creakily out of his seat to shake them both warmly by the hand. She felt so dizzy that it was a wonder her legs still supported her. Various items in the window – a tapestry stool, a brass lamp, a whole dinner-service — floated in front of her eyes.

Mum *was* in France. Dad was on his way.

What did it mean? He didn't say he'd *found* Mum. But surely he must know where to go? France was a big country. He couldn't just get there and wander about, aimlessly searching.

He must have found out something.

She tried a phone call, but there was no answer; she left a breathless message. 'Dad? Phone me as soon as you can.'

Paris? Was he going to Paris? But if Mum was there with her Other Man, Pascal Gaultier, what would happen then? Would there be a fight? A duel? And what if Mum didn't *want* to come back? After all, she could have come home, any time she chose, in the last two weeks ... and she *hadn't* chosen. Was it too late? Would she choose Dad now?

The chess box was on Mr Fotheringay's desk, and he was examining one of the pieces. Aunt Rose watched him, hands clasped as if in prayer. Aunt Nell looked round for Nina, and beckoned her in.

'Just exquisite,' Mr Fotheringay was saying. 'Such fine detail. Wonderful craftsmanship. Ravishing. I've never seen anything like it.'

Nina was bursting to tell her aunts about Dad's message, but this wasn't the time. She balanced on one foot, then the other, while Mr Fotheringay produced a magnifying glass from his desk drawer and gave the green king an even more thorough examination.

'I must say, it does look rather special, doesn't it?' Aunt Rose twittered. 'I'm a complete ignoramus, as you know, Maurice, but even I can see ... wonderful ... village way up in the mountains, she said ...'

Aunt Nell tutted. '*Do* stop clucking, dear, and let the poor man concentrate.'

Next, Mr Fotheringay took out all the pieces, peering closely at each one, and setting them in their places on the board. Then he looked at the aunts and Nina over the top of his half-moon glasses. 'I'll need to do some research into this, to be quite sure, but I think you've got something very special here. Very special indeed. I shall do some internet searching tonight.'

'Thank you, Maurice ... Ooh, how exciting!' Aunt Rose exclaimed.

'Oh, one other thing,' Mr Fotheringay said, as they left. 'That teddy bear you brought in, Rose. I've put it in tomorrow's auction. It might fetch ten or twenty pounds – I doubt more than that. We'll put our hopes on this chess set.'

'That bear!' Aunt Nell sniffed, closing the door behind her. 'I *told* you it was nothing special.'

'Still, dear,' said Aunt Rose, 'ten or twenty pounds isn't to be sneezed at, is it?'

Back at Second-Hand Rose, Nina checked her phone to find a message from Cat.

Email back from PG! Don't worry, he sez Miranda's safe.

But what did that mean? At once Nina went out to the back yard, out of the aunts' hearing, and phoned Cat, trying to tease out every nuance. Were those Pascal Gaultier's exact words? Was that all? Safe *where*? Nina already knew Mum was safe – as in alive and well – as she'd been sending messages. Pascal Gaultier's email didn't solve the problem; in fact it made it worse, especially when a message arrived from Mum herself soon after, saying **Please don't worry. I'll explain everything.** So Pascal must have told her, and that meant she was with him, which didn't bode well at all.

So what about Dad? How did he fit in? Never had an evening passed more slowly. Every few moments, Nina tried phoning Dad, in a torment of frustration. Why wasn't his phone turned on?

At last, just when she thought she'd go mad with not knowing, the aunts' phone rang.

'You get that, dear,' said Aunt Rose. 'It might be Dad.'

It was.

'Precious, I'm on a train, on my way to Toulouse. I don't know how you guessed Brighton, and then France, but that's how I— But it's all quite complicated, so I won't tell you the whole story. Anyway, I don't know it yet, till I've … till I've found Mum and talked to her. But I'm on my way. I really am. I should be with her tomorrow.'

'Toulouse? Not Paris? And Dad – have you heard of – Pascal Gaultier?'

There was such a silence that Nina thought the line had gone dead; then Dad said, in a rather unbelieving voice, 'Yes. Yes, I have! But how did *you* hear of him?'

Nina explained about the folded note in Mum's elephant bag, the address, and Dad said, 'Oh, if only we'd found that earlier! Well done, Nina.'

'Is everything OK, Dad?' she asked cautiously. He didn't sound angry, as she might have expected. He didn't sound like a man steeling himself to confront a hated rival.

'I think so, sweetheart. I really do. I'll phone you tomorrow.'

Nina took a deep breath. 'Do you promise?'

'I promise.'

❦

16

The Wicker Chair

———◆◆◆———

On Saturday, as soon as she opened her eyes, Nina felt a rush of excitement – today Dad would be with Mum. They'd be together. Surely, surely, he'd persuade her to come home; Mum couldn't let him come back on his own! Through the attic window Nina could see sunshine outside; bright, confident sunshine that looked likely to stay all day.

She was up and dressed early, impatient for her aunts and Uncle Derek to finish breakfast.

'Toast, Nina? Honey?'

It was all she could do to chomp her way through a bowl of cornflakes, but the grown-ups were behaving exactly as usual. It might have been a day like any other.

Their arrival at the shop was the same as last week: bags and boxes left in the doorway, and Aunt Rose saying: 'Tch! I *wish* people wouldn't *do* that. Why don't they read the notice?'

Unexpectedly, Jake was outside, beanie hat pulled

161

down over his hair. 'Can't come Monday. So I'm here today instead.'

'Where are you going on Monday?' Nina asked, but Jake only smiled, and picked up a bag in each hand.

He was bringing in the last one, and Aunt Rose had just changed the sign on the door to OPEN, when Mr Fotheringay appeared, carrying a small chair with curvy legs and a wickerwork seat.

'Good morning, good morning, everyone! Rose, I've brought the chair you were asking about.' He put it down near the till, and stood panting slightly.

'Thank you.' Aunt Rose hurried over. 'Nina, come and see! Mr Fotheringay's giving us this, to replace the one you broke. Oh, perfect! It's lovely, isn't it? Better, really, than the other one. Thank you, Maurice, how very kind!'

Nina was about to thank Mr Fotheringay, too, when she noticed that he didn't look at all well. His mouth opened as if he were trying to speak, but no words came out. He lurched on his feet, almost falling. His face had gone lopsided, and his eyes looked ... frightened. Frightened and confused.

'Are you all right, Maurice?' said Aunt Rose, in a fluster. 'What is it, a dizzy turn? Here, sit down.' She patted the wicker seat, and Mr Fotheringay slumped on it so heavily that Nina feared this chair might splinter and break, just like the other one. He clutched at his

162

right arm. When he tried to speak, only a gargling noise came out.

'Nina, could you fetch a glass of water?' said Aunt Nell.

Nina hurried to the kitchen. By the time she came back, Mr Fotheringay seemed to have recovered, and looked almost himself – rather embarrassed at what had happened.

'I'm so sorry,' he was saying. 'I don't know what came over me.'

'Sit and rest for a while,' urged Aunt Rose, 'and I'll make you a nice cup of tea.'

'That's very kind, but I must get back and open my shop.' Mr Fotheringay made to stand up.

'No!' said Jake loudly. 'Sit down.'

Everyone turned to look at him. It was unlike Jake to speak at all in a group of people, let alone to give orders.

'Ambulance. Call one. Ambulance.' Jake was trembling with determination. 'Now.'

Mr Fotheringay gave a huffing laugh. 'No, really, dear boy, I assure you I don't need—'

'Yes. You do.'

Aunt Nell was looking doubtful, while Aunt Rose dithered to and fro in a flurry of indecision.

'I really don't want to cause any trouble,' said Mr Fotheringay.

Aunt Nell said, 'Surely, Jake, if Mr Fotheringay says

163

he's all right now then he is? We can't call the emergency services for nothing.'

Jake hesitated for a moment, then moved towards the counter, picked up the phone and keyed in three numbers. 'Ambulance, please ... Yes ... Someone's had a stroke. Yes. Crowdenbridge, Mill Street ... Second-Hand Rose. Yes, Second-Hand Rose. It's a shop.'

The aunts and Mr Fotheringay were gazing at each other in astonishment.

'A stroke?' Mr Fotheringay gave another little laugh. 'No, no, surely not. It was just a funny turn. I'll be right as rain in a few minutes.'

'Jake, dear,' said Aunt Rose, 'what makes you so sure—'

'Stroke,' he said. 'Small one. But still. A stroke. Got to get checked. Dangerous to ignore.'

'How do you know about strokes, sweetheart?' Aunt Rose asked.

'My mum,' Jake said, with a twist of his mouth. 'Died.'

'Oh, Jake, I'm so sorry!' Aunt Rose rushed up to him, and rubbed his arm.

'Three years ago. Little stroke, like that. She thought it was nothing. Then a big one,' Jake said, each sentence an effort. 'So I know the signs. Too late for my mum.' He looked at Mr Fotheringay. 'Doesn't mean you'll die. Probably won't. Need to get checked, though.'

We know so little about Jake, Nina thought.

164

Aunt Nell went to the door and turned the sign to CLOSED. 'We don't want people coming in.'

'Really! I assure you I'm absolutely fine,' Mr Fotheringay protested, but no one else felt inclined to ignore what Jake had said. Aunt Rose offered tea and cushions, and suggested a move to the storeroom, out of the view of passers-by.

In less than ten minutes, an ambulance was outside; the crew of two, a man and a woman, took over. After a few questions and five more minutes, Mr Fotheringay was inside the ambulance; Aunt Rose, too, who thought someone should go with him to the hospital, and promised to phone with news as soon as she could.

All this had caused a small drama outside, with people gathering and staring – some of them, Nina saw, clearly hoping for something catastrophic, a dash of excitement to liven up their Saturday shopping. The ambulance pulled away, and suddenly the shop felt empty. Nina and Aunt Nell looked at each other, while Jake simply continued what he'd been doing before, carrying bags through to the storeroom.

'Jake?' Aunt Nell called him back. 'Thank you. *Thank* you. You were heroic.'

Jake shrugged, and edged away.

'You heard what the paramedic said. It was a good job someone knew what to do. None of us realised how serious it could have been.'

'OK. Going downstairs now,' said Jake, with a wriggle of his shoulders.

Aunt Nell turned the door-sign to OPEN, and customers surged in. At least, Nina took them for customers, but most simply wanted to know what had happened, and Aunt Nell had to explain, several times. Luckily, Mrs Freeman was one of them, and there was nothing she enjoyed more than a medical crisis. Once she'd heard Aunt Nell's version, she took over – with embellishments of her own. A small group gathered by the bric-a-brac. 'Of course, you can't be too careful, not with strokes,' she expounded happily. 'You might think it's nothing, but a small one can lead to a bigger one and then it's really serious. I ought to know – my sister-in-law was in and out of hospital most of last year ...'

'Will he be all right?' Nina whispered to Aunt Nell.

'I expect so.' Aunt Nell gave her a hug. 'Rose will let us know as soon as she can.'

When Ivy arrived, intending only to call in but quickly rolling up her sleeves and saying she'd help out while Aunt Rose was gone, Nina went down to the cellar to see Jake. He was at the workbench as usual, sorting out a tangle of ties.

'I'm sorry about your mum,' Nina whispered. 'I didn't know.'

'Yeah. Step mum, really.'

'What about your dad?'

Jake shook his head. 'Haven't got one.'

166

'So who—' Nina had been about to say *Who looks after you,* but of course she knew that – it was the staff at Thrapston House, like Pete, who'd lent the van. Perhaps Jake was too old to need looking after for much longer; but how strange it must feel to have no one. Was that the reason for his breakdrown? She couldn't really ask, and Jake wouldn't tell her, anyway. She wanted to tell him about Dad being in France, about to find Mum – perhaps they were together *now*! – but it didn't feel right, as Jake had no parents at all. And the morning's crisis had pushed her eagerness for news into the background. She checked her mobile, before remembering that there was no signal down here. OK. So if she stayed for a bit, sorting, it meant she was more likely to find a message, her reward, when she went back upstairs.

She was stacking plates and saucers on a shelf when Aunt Nell called down the stairs. 'Nina! Your friends are here – Cat and Thea!'

Nina had forgotten they were coming. She ran up the steps.

Aunt Nell was waiting at the top. 'Rose has just phoned, too, from the hospital. She says Mr Fotheringay's having tests, but they might let him come home later.'

'Oh, good!' Nina hadn't been able to shake off the feeling that Mr Fotheringay's stroke was somehow her fault, because he'd been bringing the chair for her when it happened.

She saw Thea searching through the shoes, and Cat

by the books, when her phone rang. She snatched at it: Dad's number.

'Hi, Dad. Where are you?'

But it wasn't Dad who answered.

'Hello, Nina darling,' said Mum's voice. 'It's me.'

17

The Purple-Flowered Dress

'Mum?' It came out as a high-pitched squeak. 'Is it really you?'

'Yes, it is,' said Mum's voice in Nina's ear, 'and I'm with Dad. I'm really sorry, *really, really* sorry, to have given you so much worry. And Dad, too.'

'Are you coming home?' Nina held her breath.

'Yes, darling, we are. We're leaving on Monday, and we'll be home on Tuesday – it's a long journey. I can't wait to see you.'

'But why? Where've you— What did you—'

'There's an awful lot to explain. Far too much for me to tell you now. I'm afraid I've been very silly.'

'Silly *how*? Mum, can't you even give me a *hint*?'

'It's too complicated, really it is. I'll explain *all* of it when I get home. I promise. I'll pass you over to Dad now. Love you, Nina. Love you lots and lots and lots.'

'Love you too, Mum. Lots.'

When Dad took over, he didn't say much, only,

'Everything's all right, Nina. We'll be home soon. Tell your aunts I'll phone this evening.'

Nina stood gazing at her phone. She couldn't believe that Mum's voice had just come out of it.

'Nina?' said Aunt Nell. 'Was that—'

'It was my mum. She's coming home.'

With so much going on, Nina wasn't sure about going to Cat and Thea's house, but Aunt Nell thought it was a good idea.

'You go, dear. I've got Ivy and Jake to help me here. It'll take your mind off things, spending time with your friends.'

So Nina went outside with them into the sunshine that matched her mood; it was a golden day, full of promise. They caught the bus to Settlebank, where Cat and Thea lived in a small Victorian house with a slate-roofed porch and patterned tiles in the hallway. There were paintings and books everywhere, and five cats, all tortoiseshell and all related.

Cat had a tiny bedroom on the first floor, but Thea's was much larger, in the attic, reaching the whole length of the house. There was a large sofa here, and a desk, and boxes and boxes of clothes, all labelled UPCYCLING.

'What I want to do,' Thea explained, 'is put each outfit on its hanger, with accessories, and a label saying who's going to wear it. Then we'll work out a running order. Billy's found the perfect music to play while people are coming in! Listen, Nina.'

She played it on her laptop. Nina listened, astonished, to a song called 'Second-Hand Rose'.

'Haven't you heard it before?' Thea said, smiling at Nina's reaction. 'It's Barbra Streisand. I bet that's where your aunts got the shop name.'

Nina was doubtful, as she'd always thought the shop was named after Aunt Rose, but she made Thea play the song twice more until the tune and some of the words were firmly installed in her memory.

Soon, clothes on hangers were strung all along the ceiling beams – wonderful groupings of fabrics and colours, put together with Thea's eye for detail.

Cat was to wear a silky grey skirt with a hem that fell into points, and a cobwebby wrap top over a silver camisole. 'You can try it on, in a minute,' Thea told her sister, 'with your clumpy boots and red tights, I thought.'

Nina was beginning to feel anxious about walking out on the catwalk. She wasn't tall and elegant, like Cat. She'd feel silly and dressed up. She'd trip over. She'd make a mess of it.

'Nina,' said Thea, 'I've got a dress that's just perfect for you! I bought it ages ago, on the pound rail, before I even thought of the show. It's just right.'

'I don't think I know how to wear a dress. I nearly always wear jeans when I'm not at school.'

Nina's eyes were on the carrier bag Thea had taken

from the top of a pile, and the dress she was pulling out. In the instant before she properly saw it, Nina had a tingling feeling that it would be something of Mum's.

It was.

Mum in the garden, one hot day last summer – Nina could see her quite clearly, wearing her favourite dress, fine cotton splashed with purple flowers, the one she wore over and over again. Reaching up to pick apples, Mum had got the skirt of the dress caught in a rose-bush, and had tangled herself even more firmly trying to free herself from the thorns. The dress was badly ripped, and Mum was sad, and cross with herself. Although she tried to mend it, the thorns had shredded too much of the skirt. 'I'll give it to the shop,' Mum decided. 'Someone might like the fabric, or turn it into a blouse.'

Now someone was going to, and for Nina.

'You can wear jeans as well!' said Thea. 'It's too long and a bit droopy, as well as being torn and mended, but a lovely fabric. What I'll do is chop off most of the skirt, see.' She held it against Nina, gathering up the hem in one hand. 'And I'll take in the sleeves, and turn it into a tunic. You can wear it with skinny jeans and boots, and a bright green waistcoat I've got somewhere, and a purple rosette. What d'you think?'

'Ooh, yes!' Nina couldn't wait to see herself.

'Cool! Completely Nina,' said Cat. 'It'll look great!'

At lunchtime Cat and Thea's mum arrived home, with

172

Bill, who must be the boyfriend – though 'boyfriend' didn't seem quite the right word for someone who looked older than Dad. They'd brought delicious food from Pumpernickel, and they all had lunch in the garden, sitting at a big bench-table. This time yesterday it would have been painful for Nina to eat Pumpernickel food, with its sharp reminders of Mum, but now everything – the dress, the falafels and samosas, pitta and dips – seemed to point towards a happy reunion.

Nina's thoughts kept returning to Mum's *I'm afraid I've been very silly.* What could it mean? Eventually, when the meal was over and the others had gone inside, she couldn't help telling Cat, and asking what she thought.

'It's that Pascal Gaultier. Her other man. Definitely.' Cat was finishing a peach.

'But how does she know him?'

'From all those years ago, when she was dancing in France. He's been in love with her ever since, and wrote to her in secret.'

'But she didn't sound at all *ashamed*,' Nina pointed out. 'More *happy*.'

'That's because she knows she's made the right decision,' said Cat, licking juice from her fingers. 'Sticking with you and your dad.'

Nina couldn't help thinking that a mum who could do such a thing wouldn't be the mum she knew; the mum she'd spoken to just this morning.

Only now did she remember about the twins, and that she hadn't looked for the photo.

She told Cat, who instantly said, 'What if *you're* a twin? The photo could have been of you and your lost twin brother! Wait – what if Pascal Gaultier is really your father?'

'But Dad's my father. I can't have two.'

All the same, Nina couldn't help being rather taken with the idea of having a lost twin, even if it took a stretch of imagination to see herself as one of the boys in the photo.

'No. That doesn't work. There are baby photos of me in Mum and Dad's photo album.'

'You *think* they're of you. What if they're not? What if it's another baby – your older sister? Perhaps she got lost or died or something? Then you were born after that.'

Nina felt rather perturbed by this shake-up of the family she knew, especially later, when Max phoned back with ideas of his own. 'Your mum's gone off to see her identical twin sister. Yes, sister – they were just dressing as boys for that photo. The sister's a brilliant dancer, and she's just inherited a fortune – money and priceless jewels – from someone who saw her dance. And she decided this was the time to make up the quarrel with your mum.'

'Why did they quarrel?'

'The twin sister was in love with your dad, obviously, only he chose your mum. They haven't spoken since.

The sister's got over it now, with this new man in her life, who's just died. Only, when your mum got to France, she found it was all a hoax about the fortune and the jewels, and now she's consoling her twin.'

'Yeah, right,' Nina scoffed.

Dad's phone call that evening didn't reveal anything more, either; he just repeated what Mum had said, that there was too much to explain by phone, and that they'd soon be on their way home.

'Well, it's a mystery, for sure,' said Aunt Rose, when Dad had rung off. 'We'll just have to wait.'

❦

On Sunday, the aunts and Uncle Derek took Nina and Max to the Haworth Parsonage Museum, where the Brontë family had lived.

'It's years and years since I've been,' said Aunt Rose. 'So atmospheric. So sad. But so inspiring as well. I must phone Maurice, first, to check he's OK. And let's go and see him when we get back. I've made fat rascals.'

The golden autumn weather was continuing, but nevertheless the parsonage looked bleak, standing behind a graveyard. Inside, Nina looked at the tiny notebooks filled with minuscule handwriting, and at the table where the Brontë children had sat every evening, writing their stories and reading them to each other.

'Weren't they determined!' marvelled Aunt Rose. 'Fancy those girls having to pretend to be men, to get their books published. And how sad, all dying so young.'

'But their wonderful stories will last for ever,' Aunt Nell said. 'If only they could know.' In the gift shop she bought Nina a copy of *Jane Eyre*: 'I loved it when I wasn't much older than you. Try it now, but if you don't like it, put it aside for two or three years.'

Nina bought postcards for Jake and Cat and one for the kitchen notice board; Max chose himself a new notebook, and Aunt Rose bought a mug and a card for Mr Fotheringay.

'He's an antiques expert, dear,' Aunt Nell pointed out. 'Do you really think a mass-produced mug is quite the thing?' But Aunt Rose said it was the thought that counted.

Back at Crowdenbridge, they went to Mr Fotheringay's flat above his shop and had tea and fat rascals. Mr Fotheringay looked pale but cheerful, and was delighted with Aunt Rose's present.

'With all this enforced rest, I've had time to make plans for the chess set,' he told them. 'There's a fine art auction in two weeks, and – if you agree – I shall enter it for that. It's the best chance of getting a really good price.'

Aunt Nell was doubtful. 'But what if it doesn't?'

'Don't worry, I shall put a substantial reserve on it. I shan't let it go for less than it's worth. And I'll be very disappointed indeed if it doesn't fetch something in the region of four thousand pounds.'

'Four thousand pounds!' Aunt Rose looked quite bewildered, as if she'd never heard of such an amount.

'At least,' said Mr Fotheringay. 'Now, I'd like your advice, please. I owe a great deal to that excellent young man, Jake, for his quick thinking. I've had a scare, but thanks to him I know what to look out for in future. I'd like to give him something to say thank you – but what would you recommend?'

Aunt Rose clasped her hands together. 'Oh, Maurice, what a kind thought! But what should it be? Nina, you talk quite a lot to Jake. What do you think he'd like?'

Nina could only think *a car*, but she didn't imagine Mr Fotheringay was talking about that sort of money. She thought hard.

'He likes animals. Dogs. And especially llamas.'

'Does he really?' said Mr Fotheringay. 'Llamas? Well, well.'

'A bike!' Nina said, remembering. 'He wants a bike.'

Mr Fotheringay looked pleased. 'That would certainly be easier to get than a llama.'

※

It had been a good day, Nina decided later, getting ready for bed. And now she was a day nearer to Mum and Dad coming home, with the missing puzzle pieces she'd been looking for.

18

The China Seahorse

———◆———

Nina was slow to get dressed after PE on Monday, and Cat, wanting to return her library book during break, had gone on ahead. Leaving the changing room, Nina saw Jem and Tash by the notice board next to the PE office. They were talking about the Upcycling Show poster, but as soon as Jem saw Nina, her manner changed.

'Oh, look, here she is,' said Jem. 'Second-Hand Rose herself. Cat says you're in this. What is it, a load of old tat from that manky shop you go to? Wow. Hold me back.'

'Don't come then, if that's what you think.' Nina tried to walk past, but Jem stepped in front of her.

'Oh, we wouldn't miss it for anything. It'll be good for a laugh, won't it, Tash? Nee-nah trying to look like a supermodel, in scrotty old clothes?'

'Will your weirdo friend be in it?' Tash asked. 'I've got to see that.'

'*What* weirdo friend?' Nina could only think she meant Cat.

'That guy who works there. The one you hang out with.' Jem mimed pulling a hat down over her eyes; she slumped, letting her arms hang low.

'I don't know who you mean.'

'Yes, you do. He lives at that loony house, doesn't he? He's one of those retards. *Hello, Neeeena. You're my fwend.*'

Nina stared, realising that they were talking about Jake. At least, they thought they were, but Jake didn't talk like that, or resemble a gorilla any more than any other human being did.   She felt herself going hot.

'Aw, Jem – you're making her blush, look!'

'If you mean Jake,' Nina said, trying to sound haughty, though she knew her cheeks had flamed scarlet, 'you need to know that he's one of the nicest, kindest people I know. Yes, he *is* my friend. A good friend. And ...' she made herself taller '... he's a *hero*. He practically saved someone's life on Saturday.'

She should have known better.

'Oo! Oo! Look at me, I'm a hero!' Jem chanted, even more gorilla-ish now, bending her knees and beating her chest with both fists. Tash burst into loud, cackling laughter.

'You're sick, you two! This is complete rubbish. I haven't got time for any more.' Nina sidestepped them, and marched away, head high.

Behind her, she heard yells of, 'Ooo, Jake! Jake, you're such a hero!' Then a door was flung open and the voice of Mr Bailey, Head of PE, rang out into the sudden hush.

'What's this vile noise? Is someone strangling a cat?'

'Oh, nothing, sir. We were just messing about.'

Nina smirked at the quick change of tone. But she was still burning with anger on Jake's behalf. And, as she headed for the library, she imagined herself on the catwalk in the outfit that was just *her*, and how stupid she'd feel if Jem and Tash were sniggering in the front row.

❧

'Aunt Rose,' Nina remembered to ask, later, 'did you know there's a *song* called Second-Hand Rose?'

'Yes, dear, of course,' Aunt Rose said promptly. 'Barbra Streisand. *Funny Girl.* That's why we gave the shop its name.'

'Oh! I thought it was because *you're* Second-Hand Rose.'

'Well, it's both. The perfect name for the shop.' Aunt Rose started to sing it, forgetting some of the words.

'No, I don't think that's right, Aunt. It's *clothes,* not *bows.* But actually, *bows* makes a better rhyme with *Rose.*'

There was no stopping Aunt Rose now. She inflated her lungs, and swelled into the singing, performing to an invisible audience. When she reached the end, she gave a sweeping curtsey and pretended to accept a bouquet of flowers.

'Very nice, Rose, dear,' said Aunt Nell. 'But I think that's enough, don't you?'

Nina realised that something was missing: the green crocodile. She thought one of her aunts might have moved it, but Aunt Rose said, 'No, dear. It's gone again. Someone bought it this morning.'

Nina was disappointed, but before she had time to think much about it, Max came in, on his way to play chess with Mr Fotheringay.

'With that special Chinese chess set,' he explained. 'Mr Fotheringay thought it should play at least one game before it goes off to auction.'

Footsteps clomped up the cellar stairs, and Jake emerged with a collection of men's tops and shirts, ready on hangers. He said hello to Max, looked around to see that no customers were in the shop, then said, 'Er, I've … I've … I've … got a job. Um. Start Monday.'

Aunt Rose nearly dropped a teapot she was pricing. 'Really, sweetheart? That's marvellous. Where is it?'

'With the llamas.'

'Llamas?' echoed Aunt Nell.

'Yeah.' Jake smiled his most dazzling smile. 'Julie's assistant's leaving. This week. She's giving me the job.'

'At Lumberforth Llamas? That's brilliant,' said Nina.

'Cool!' Max gave a big thumbs-up. 'But how will you get there? It's miles out on the moors.'

'Live there. On the farm. Flat above the stables.'

'Oh, Jake darling, that's absolutely wonderful!' Aunt

181

Rose moved towards him for a big hug; he recoiled, then let her embrace him. 'But ... does this mean we're losing you? You won't come any more?'

'Thought I would. One day a week,' said Jake. 'Mondays. If that's OK. If I can borrow a bike.' He shuffled his feet, embarrassed. 'I like it here.'

'And we love having you, Jake. If you can manage it, we'd be delighted,' Aunt Nell told him.

The aunts hadn't heard of Lumberforth Llamas, so between them Nina, Jake and Max explained: about the trekking, about how good it was for people, especially nervous or stressed people, to be with llamas, learning to handle them, gaining confidence. Jake would be looking after the llamas, and helping the people who visited.

'Helping *people*, dear?' Aunt Nell said doubtfully. 'You're always so reluctant to come up here when there are people about.'

'Jake will be fine,' Nina told her, 'when he's with llamas. He's so good with them! They make all the difference.'

Embarrassed at so much attention, Jake went downstairs again.

When she was sure he'd gone, Aunt Rose whispered to Nina, 'That teddy-bear – it was his, you know.'

'What – the one you took to Mr Fotheringay?'

Aunt Rose nodded. 'Jake asked me about it, and he went bright red, the dear boy, and I guessed. It would have been awful to throw it in the skip.'

'So why did he give it away?'

Aunt Rose beamed. 'I think it's a good sign, dear, don't you? He's ready to move on to a new stage of his life. And now this lovely job has come along. Perfect, just perfect.'

❦

Mum and Dad were getting closer. They'd driven all the way up to the ferry port of Caen, and were sailing on an overnight ferry. They would arrive at Portsmouth early in the morning, then make the long journey up the motorways to Yorkshire. Allowing for stops, Dad thought they'd be home by the time Nina finished school.

Nina was in a fidget of anticipation. Nothing could go wrong now, could it? But, instantly, her imagination produced a selection of obstacles. There might be a strike, and the ferry wouldn't sail. Or the boat might capsize. Or be hijacked. Mum might fall overboard. Even if they did get safely to Portsmouth, someone might have smuggled drugs into Mum's suitcase, and she'd be caught and arrested.

Luckily, none of those things *did* happen. At lunchtime on Tuesday Nina got a text from Dad: **Don't get bus CU @ sch g8s.**

The school gates! Nina smiled, and texted back **Cool.**

She floated through the school day in a dream, hardly aware of which lessons she was having. Cat covered up for her more than once, and, in French, passed a helpful note when Nina was called upon to ask for groceries in a shop.

At last the day was at an end. 'Have a great evening! Tell me all about it tomorrow,' said Cat, hurrying off to the bus bays. Nina jogged towards the gate, weaving round groups of slow drifters, her eyes scanning ahead.

Yes! There was Dad, waving, and ... there was Mum, beside him.

Really Mum! Here! In person! Mum!

She looked much the same as always – hair twisted up messily, a sparkly scarf wrapped round her shoulders and pinned with one of her own fabric rosettes. She was a little more tanned than she'd been before; that was the only change Nina could see.

Nina ran up to them. Mum opened her arms wide and wrapped her in a great hug, and after a moment Dad joined in, too.

'Oh, Nina, darling, I've missed you so much!' Mum exclaimed.

'Me, too.' Nina's mouth was muffled by Mum's scarf. She smelled Mum's lovely patchouli smell.

'We thought we'd go straight home,' said Dad, 'and later we'll go round to the aunts', to collect your things.'

'Mum, are you all right?' Nina had to keep staring, to make sure Mum wouldn't prove to be a mirage, melting into air.

'Yes, Nina – perfectly, perfectly all right, and so *happy*. What's more important is – how are *you*?'

At home, things began to seem oddly normal. Dad brought Mum's case in, and picked up two letters from the mat; Mum unpacked the shopping they'd bought on the way, and they all sat at the kitchen table with mugs of tea. Nina had asked the aunts if she could bring Mum's china seahorse back (she planned to find something else for their bathroom) and now she took it out of her bag and placed it in the centre of the table.

'Nina, thank you! I was going to give it to Tiffany, but maybe I'll keep it, and buy her flowers instead. And my bag, too – I'm so glad you rescued that. Oh, it's lovely to be back home! The three of us together, just as it should be.'

Nina looked at her expectantly. 'Well, *you're* the one who—'

'Go on,' said Dad. 'I think Nina's waited long enough, don't you?'

'Right.' Mum took a deep breath. 'Nina, darling, there's something I've never told you. Or Dad, till a few days ago. I know you've always wondered why Dad and I aren't married. There's a very good reason why I couldn't marry him, and it's not because I don't love him, or because I don't love you. Certainly not that.'

'What, then?'

'The reason is,' Mum said, 'that I was married already.'

For a few giddy moments, Nina felt that the room was tilting around her, the chair trying to tip her to the floor. She tried to speak, but produced only a feeble sound, something between a gasp and a hiccup.

'To someone else,' Mum added.

Nina's mouth was open. She closed it, swallowed, and managed a few words: 'But ... How? What?'

'I'll tell you the whole story, sweetheart. Right from the start.'

19

The Jewelled Evening Purse

———◆———

'I wasn't very happy as a little girl. I lived with just my mother until I was twelve. She was always either at work or out with friends, and didn't have much time for me. Then she married a man I was supposed to call my stepfather. Soon they had a baby of their own, and I felt in the way.

'What I always loved was dancing. There was a teacher at my school who ran a dance club, and that was where I felt free, where I could really be myself. As soon as I was old enough, I left school and trained as a dancer, and started to get work. I wasn't good enough for lead roles, but I did get regular work, usually with touring companies. Most of my time was spent on the road, travelling from place to place, dancing in small theatres, staying in guesthouses with the other dancers. It wasn't glamorous, and it certainly wasn't well paid, but it was fun.

'I hardly ever went home. My mother and I sent postcards to each other now and then, but soon we stopped bothering. I did send her a postcard when I got married, but that was the last one. So, when I say that I've got no family, Nina, it's not strictly true. I've got a mother in Brighton—'

'*Brighton!*' Nina looked at Dad, who gave a small nod. 'That's right, Nina,' he said. 'It was you sending me to Brighton that eventually led me to Mum.'

'I've also got a half-brother I haven't seen since he was a toddler,' said Mum. 'Maybe I ought to – but, anyway … One of my dancing jobs took me to France, touring. That was exciting! My first time abroad. We stopped in various cities, including Toulouse. It was there I met Armand Beauregard.'

'Armand – d'you mean he's the one you …' Nina was confused. 'Not Pascal, then, Pascal Gaultier?'

'No, no, not Pascal! I don't know how you got his name, but he was very surprised to get your email.'

'I found a slip of paper in your elephant bag, with his email address on it.'

'Oh! Well, that's because … But I'll tell you later. Armand was a theatre director in Toulouse, and we were performing in his show. He specialised in dance productions. He was in his late twenties, a good few years older than me – I was nineteen at the time. He was handsome, in a very French way – beautiful manners, very flattering, and especially flattering to me. When I danced I'd glimpse him in the wings, and he'd always be watching me, as if I were the only dancer on the stage. He invited me out for dinner, he sent me roses, and before long I was falling in love. I'd never had that sort of attention. I was swept off my feet.'

Nina glanced at Dad, but he didn't seem to mind hearing all this.

'So you married him?' she asked. 'Did you stay in France?'

'Yes. The touring company moved on, and I said goodbye to the friends I'd made, and stayed with Armand in Toulouse. He'd been married before, and he had children – twin boys, Alain and Adrien …'

The photograph! The two boys!

'What, darling?' Mum asked, smiling.

'No, go on. I'll tell you later.'

Mum nodded, and continued. 'Their mother, Chantelle, was another dancer. When she and Armand were divorced, she left the twins with him, so it became my job to look after them. They were lovely, lovely boys, but I had to learn fast. I'd expected to carry on dancing, but Armand didn't like seeing me on the stage in skimpy costumes now that I was his wife. And somehow the boys took up all my time.'

Nina frowned. 'So really he wanted you as a babysitter?'

'That's what Dad says,' said Mum, with a sidelong look and smile at him. 'But, at the time … well, I felt very lucky, and thought I'd go back to dancing when the boys were a bit older. Armand and I were waiting for a baby of our own, and we both hoped for a little girl. But it didn't happen. Of course I thought it must be *my* fault, because he'd already proved he could father children. He started to blame me, too. The marriage wasn't turning out quite as I'd expected. Then another theatre company arrived, and soon he was flirting with the prettiest actress. That happened again and again, while I mostly stayed at home with the twins, and wondered what lies he was telling me.' Mum looked down at the table. 'But, well, who am I to talk about telling lies? I've told too many lies myself. Or, at least, never told the truth.'

'So what happened? To you and him?'

'I was with him for three years, by which time I was thinking I'd made a bad mistake. Then, the last straw – Chantelle took the boys back to live with her in Paris. I was heartbroken – I couldn't have missed them more if they'd been my own babies. Without them, I couldn't face staying with Armand any more. So, I packed my bags one night while he was at the theatre, and ran away. I caught a train to Paris and crossed the Channel and came back to England.'

'Didn't Armand come after you?'

'There was no way I could know whether he did or not. I made sure I left no trace. I didn't leave a note. The only person I told was Pascal.'

'Pascal!'

'Pascal was Armand's assistant. Still is. I got on well

with him, and his office was in the house, so we often used to chat together and play with the twins. I couldn't leave without at least saying goodbye. But I only said I was leaving – I didn't say where I was going. I didn't go back to Brighton. I headed for London, worked as a waitress, tried to get auditions – and eventually got a job with another dance company. I tried to forget all about Armand. I didn't miss him at all – it was the twins I missed, Alain and Adrien. And I felt really guilty that I'd left without telling them.'

'Did you ever see them again?'

'Not till last week! They're eighteen now, handsome young men, about to go off to university. But we're getting too far ahead.'

Nina nodded. 'You haven't got to you and Dad, yet.'

She knew something of this part of the story – how Mum had been dancing at a theatre where Dad was stage carpenter. How Dad had seen Mum in rehearsals, and thought how attractive she was, then helped her one day when – typical Mum! – she'd lost her keys and her money. 'I thought she'd have loads of boyfriends waiting at the stage door,' he'd told Nina. 'I never thought for a minute she'd be interested in me.'

'I didn't expect to meet anyone else. Didn't even want to,' Mum said now. 'I just wanted to be myself. But then I met this charming young man ...' she looked coyly at Dad '... at the theatre in Bradford, and he was so nice, and so honest, and so straightforward – such a lovely contrast to the life I'd been leading. I loved spending time with him. We started off as friends, but I wasn't going to tell anyone, not even Richard, about France and my marriage to Armand. I was too ashamed of what I'd done. So whenever he asked me about myself, about my family, I hardly told him anything at all – only about my dancing and my ambitions, and some of the places I'd visited on tour. I never meant to lie. I probably *didn't* lie, much. I just left out large parts of the truth.'

'You *did* lie,' Dad reminded her. 'You told me you grew up in Devon. And that your parents had both died. It was such a touchy subject that you never wanted to talk about it, so I stopped asking.'

Mum bit her lip. 'Yes. Sorry. I don't know why I did that. It just came out, and I had to keep pretending for so long that I nearly believed it myself.'

'So, Dad, you never knew about Mum's … Mum's …' Nina couldn't make herself say the word *husband*. She just couldn't.

Dad shook his head. 'I had no idea, Nina. No more than you did.'

'Why didn't you ever tell?'

'Well.' Mum gave a sigh. 'We were friends at first. But then we both realised – at the same time, I think – we were falling in love. I kept thinking, *I'll have to tell him. Tomorrow, I'll tell him.* But somehow the time was never right. And then it seemed too late. And I was scared of losing him, Nina, if he knew. So I kept quiet. I thought

192

– I really thought, and it was stupid, I know – if I put Armand right out of my mind, it was as if he'd never existed. It was Richard and me, now. Here was my chance of happiness.'

Dad took hold of Mum's hand, while Nina puzzled at something in this that made no sense at all.

'But I still don't see … What made you go back to France in such a hurry? To Toulouse? Was it to see Armand? Why *now*, if you'd tried so hard to forget him?'

'I had a message from Pascal,' Mum said, 'telling me that Armand had had a serious accident and might not survive. He had a fall – in the theatre. They were rehearsing a show that involved dancers suspended from wires, high above the stage, and he'd gone up to the rigging platform to see for himself how it worked, when he lost his balance and fell. He was in hospital, in intensive care – it looked as if he might *die*. Pascal thought I should know, because he knew how bad I'd felt about running away.' She took a deep breath. 'When I heard, I went into a panic. All the guilt and the bad feeling came flooding back, and I just had to go and see him. This might be the last chance I'd ever have to say goodbye, to say sorry for leaving the way I did.'

'If only you'd *told* me,' Dad said gently, shaking his head. 'If only you'd told me then.'

'I know. I was so stupid.' Mum looked down. 'A nasty little part of me was thinking that if he died – if Armand died – I'd be properly free. I don't mean that I *wanted* him to die. I just thought *if.* It was really horrible of me, I know that.'

'*Did* he die?' Nina whispered.

'No, darling, he didn't. By the time I got there, he was starting to move a little. He's broken several bones, but he's out of intensive care now.'

'So, all these years,' Nina said, 'all the time you've been with Dad – and my whole life – you've been married to Armand? You're *still* married to him?'

Mum looked at Dad. 'I thought I was. But when I got to Toulouse, I found that Armand's wife was with him. His *third* wife, Paulette.'

'His wife! How could he get married again if—'

'I know. I was shocked. And *relieved.* I've been so silly, Nina, in all sorts of ways. I know so little about how things work, and I didn't think to find out. If you leave someone the way I did, and disappear from their lives, they can divorce you. You don't have to be there to agree or disagree. That's what Armand did. He divorced me in my absence so that he could marry Paulette.'

'So you're *not* married any more.'

'No. All this time I thought I was still married to him,' Mum said, 'but, after all, I'm not. He divorced me ten years ago.'

'So there's nothing to stop you from marrying Dad!'

Nina looked from one to the other; at their happy-sad faces full of concern for each other and for her, at their shiny eyes.

Mum and Dad exchanged smiles, and Mum gave a little laugh. 'Well, no, there isn't! But are you OK, Nina? I'm dying to hear all *your* news about school, and the shop, and the aunts.'

'Wait, though,' Nina said, still puzzling. 'What I still don't understand is how Pascal got in touch with you. How did he know your address? And what about the things that turned up in the shop? The elephant bag, and the beady purse with cufflinks in it, and the photo? The twins – I've seen their picture.'

'Oh, Nina!' exclaimed Mum. 'Did you find that? I've been looking everywhere for Armand's special cufflinks.'

20

The Tweed Cap

<hr />

Dad had the idea of buying a fish-and-chip supper for everyone, with vegetable samosas for Mum, and taking it round to the aunts and Uncle Derek. The aunts warmed the plates and put out tomato sauce and vinegar, and Uncle Derek poured drinks, and Mum and Nina unwrapped the portions, and it felt like a feast.

Of course, a lot of things had to be explained all over again, and Nina couldn't help remembering that Aunt Nell had been doubtful about Mum, calling her *a flighty piece, head in the clouds,* and not good enough for Dad. But no one could doubt Dad's delight at having Mum back, or hers at being here, and she hadn't been as bad as everyone thought, had she? Yes, there was another man – but a long-ago man, before she and Dad had even met.

Mum was still Mum, even if there was a lot to get used to.

'But how did you work it all out, Richard, dear?'

Aunt Rose was full of admiration. 'How did you find your way to Toulouse?'

Dad explained how he'd gone from one of Mum's friends to another: from Savitra in the Lake District to Alex in Sheffield, a choreographer from Mum's dancing days. She'd suggested Clare in Sussex; then Nina had thought of Brighton, and when he mentioned Brighton to Clare she remembered that Mum had worked for a month in Rokshana's Indian clothes shop. Indigo Moon wasn't there any more, but after a lot of asking around Dad had eventually found Rokshana, now using her real name, Rita, and running a guesthouse in Hove. Rita told him that Mum's mother lived in Brighton, but that she and Mum hadn't spoken for years. This was news to Dad, who wondered if the mother was still there. He looked up *Flyte* in the phone directory, found just one, and turned up on the doorstep of a house near the station.

'My goodness,' exclaimed Aunt Nell. 'What a complicated trail!'

'So – that was my *grandmother*,' Nina said, only just realising this. 'Will I meet her?'

'I think Nina ought to, don't you?' Dad said to Mum, who was silent for a moment before nodding, and saying, 'Yes. We'll all go and see her.'

'What did she say, when you turned up?' Aunt Rose asked.

'Well, that was when I got the biggest shock,' Dad said.

'I told her I was looking for Miranda, and she said "Is it about that letter that came? About Miranda's husband in France?" Husband! I started to say no, and explain who I was, but then it hit me, what she was saying. You could have knocked me over with a feather duster.'

'Oh, poor Richard!' said Aunt Nell, looking at Mum with a hint of reproach.

'Actually, I went so pale and faint that she had to ask me in. She said she hadn't known what to do with the letter – *she* had no idea where Miranda was – so she'd put it in the paper recycling. It was just lucky that the recycling collection wasn't till the next week.'

'And that must have been from Pascal?' said Nina.

'It was,' said Mum. 'He knew that I'd lived in Brighton as a child. So he did the same as Dad – searched the online phone directory, and there she was, my mother. He phoned at first, three times, but my mum's never been good at listening – she thought he was trying to sell her something, and put the phone down. That's why he sent the letter. Then he found my name on Tiffany's website and wrote to me there, as well.'

'Oh! It's so exciting.' Aunt Rose's knife and fork were propped against her plate, eating forgotten. 'So *romantic*. That was very clever of you, Richard, dear, and Nina too, and so devoted of you to go chasing over to France.' She caught Aunt Nell's eye. 'I don't mean exciting that the poor man's lying injured in hospital, dear. No, I don't mean that at all.'

'Don't let your fish and chips go cold,' Aunt Nell told her. 'Cold chips aren't at all appetising.'

'Did you actually *meet* Armand, Dad?' Nina asked. 'That must have been weird.'

'Yes, it was a bit. I wasn't looking forward to it. But it's hard to take a dislike to someone who's lying in a hospital bed with his leg on a hoist. And the really good thing is that Mum met the twins, and so did I.'

'Will you see them again?' Uncle Derek asked Mum.

'I hope so! They're in Paris. Not nearly so far as Toulouse.'

'Will *I* meet them?' Nina asked.

'I don't see why not. Maybe we should all go to Paris. Or invite them to stay with us. They've never been to England.'

It seemed the sort of evening when anything was possible. Nina speared the last of her chips, thinking how peculiar this was. She'd so often dreamed of having a brother or a sister, and now – OK, Alain and Adrien weren't her brothers, weren't related to her at all, but it could be the next best thing. And she even had a grandmother and a half-uncle as well!

'Nina, sweetheart, we're going to miss you!' Aunt Rose was beginning to look a bit overcome. 'It's been lovely having you stay with us.'

'Thank you for having me. It's been brilliant.' Nina found that – in spite of all the worry – she'd enjoyed it. But now she was going home, *home*, and would sleep in her own bed, so she couldn't really share Aunt Rose's regret.

'You can come again, Nina,' said Uncle Derek. 'Whenever you like.'

'I'm sorry about your evening purse, Miranda,' Aunt Nell was saying. 'I'm afraid we've sold it. I could, I suppose, ask for it back, as it shouldn't have been in the shop – that does happen, sometimes.'

'Oh, no, please don't worry,' Mum assured her. 'It's not the bag that's important, only the things in it. The cufflinks, especially. They were Armand's – given to him by his father. Quite valuable, I should think.'

'We've got those,' said Aunt Nell. 'They're locked in the counter drawer.'

'Yes, Nina told me. I didn't even know I had them till I started packing. I was looking for the evening purse because I knew the photograph was in it, and then I found the cufflinks as well, in the inner pocket. I felt like a thief! I'd had them for all those years and not known. I remember, vaguely, coming home one hot night from a party, just before I ran away, and Armand taking them off and giving them to me to look after. So now was my chance to take them back. It wasn't Richard's fault the wrong things ended up in the shop. It was my own muddle. I'd been having a good clear-out, and I put some old clothes in the wardrobe, and when I started packing in secret I put those things there, too. I knew which was which, but Richard didn't.'

'Just trying to be helpful,' said Dad.

'I know. And thanks to that customer being honest, the cufflinks came back. *And* Nina rescued my elephant bag. Those are the things that matter most. I'll pack the cufflinks very carefully and post them to Armand, with a letter to explain.'

'Mum,' said Nina, pushing her plate away. 'You won't do that again, will you? Run away without telling us?'

Mum and Dad looked at each other; Mum smiled. 'No, Nina. I'll never do that again. I promise.'

❦

Nina ought to have been able to concentrate properly on her lessons now, but the Upcycling Show was so close that she couldn't stop thinking about it. Neither could anyone else. There were posters all over school, Thea and her friends had done a presentation in assembly, and tickets were selling fast. Thea had been interviewed on West Yorkshire Radio, and there were even rumours that local television might pick up the story.

Mum was intrigued by the idea of a show that combined fashion with recycling. 'What a fabulous idea! I'll definitely come – you too, Richard? Yes, let's all go. I must meet this Thea – she sounds very enterprising. And your new friend, Cat.'

Nina was to make her catwalk appearance alongside Cat and a boy from Year Nine called Linus. 'You three are the youngest in the show, so we'll give you a little scene of your own,' Thea explained, and played them the boppy music Billy had chosen. She wanted them to run and skip out, then do cartwheels. Nina and Cat practised on the games field at lunchtimes, and soon cartwheeling became quite a craze in Year Seven.

At the rehearsal, Preeyul reported that tickets had sold out completely. 'We're going to ask for another row of seats, but after that it'll be standing room only.'

While Nina was hanging up her clothes on the rail, with her name-tag, she saw someone come into the hall and sidle up to Thea. It was Tash, with Jem just behind. Nina didn't hear what they said, but she heard Thea's reply: 'No, everything's worked out, and this is the final run-through. I did put out a notice at the start of term – you could have joined in then if you'd wanted to, but it's too late now. Sorry. There are a few tickets left if you'd like to come on the night.'

Ha! So they wanted to be in the show, now, after all they'd said about mank and tat! Nina felt smug; they weren't laughing at her now.

There were mutterings in the form-room. ''S'not fair! Cat Claws and Second-Hand Rose are only in it cos Cat's sister's the organiser!'

'Yes! Of course that's the reason!' Cat agreed loudly, deflating Jem and Tash so successfully that they had to keep any further complaints to themselves.

❧

There was such a buzz on Thursday evening that when Nina peeped out from behind the curtain her stomach went whirly with anticipation. Mum and Dad were there somewhere, with the aunts and Uncle Derek, though she couldn't see them in the pool of faces.

'You'll be fine.' Cat came up behind, and tipped Nina's cap so that it tilted over her eyes. Nina loved this cap, the finishing touch to her outfit: Thea had customised an ordinary tweed cap, the sort old men wore in the street, by adding ribbon trim in green and purple velvet, and a large purple rosette on one side. Nina wore it with her hair tucked up inside, liking the cheeky look it gave her.

When the music started, 'Second-Hand Rose', Aunt Rose's special song, Nina couldn't resist sneaking another look to see if her aunts were in sight. Yes, there they were, making their way along a middle row; Nina saw Aunt Rose turn to the front of the hall in delighted surprise. For a cringe-making moment, Nina feared that she'd burst into full-throated song, joining Barbra Streisand in an unmelodious duet. Luckily Aunt Nell was there, close behind, ushering Aunt Rose into her seat and making her sit down demurely.

Giggling, Nina saw three more people coming in at the back. Max was first; then Mr Fotheringay, who looked round and beckoned to the person behind him.

'Jake!' Nina whispered.

Yes, really Jake, with his collar turned up and his beanie hat pulled down low. He stopped in the doorway, holding the frame for support. He seemed to be taking deep breaths. Then he walked right in, and followed Max and Mr Fotheringay to the only spare seats in the back row.

'See that man over there with the camera?' Cat pointed. 'Thea says he's from Pennine TV. We're going to be on television!'

Nina felt more nervous than ever. What if she messed up, in front of the camera?

Thea pulled them both back, out of sight. 'OK, everyone.' She turned to face the first six people, who were standing ready. 'The hall's packed out! And we're ready for them. It'll be brilliant. Enjoy!'

The lights dimmed, and Barbra Streisand's voice faded. Billy cued in the next track, and Thea stepped out, the spotlight following her. Nina and Cat huddled in darkness, listening to her voice on the sound system. She sounded full of confidence, as if she did this all the time.

'Hello, everyone, and welcome to our Upcycling Show – a fashion show with a difference. Everything you see here is recycled – or *up*cycled – apart from a few things that are Model's Own, as they say in magazines. Upcycling? It means you take something thrown out, something that might be seen as useless or outdated or ripped or threadbare or broken – and with a little imagination and a bit of effort you turn it into something new and useful and exciting. In this case, you make it into something that's great to wear. Our gorgeous girls and boys will be modelling everything from street clothes to office outfits, from sportswear to ballgowns. The difference from other fashion shows is that there's only one of each garment – lots of them will be on sale after the show, so get in quickly if you're interested! And we hope to give you ideas of your own, and send you flocking to the nearest charity shops and car-boot sales. Everyone benefits – you can make an outfit that's totally unique, totally yours, and save yourself a fortune at the same time. That's enough from me – enjoy the show!'

It was happening! The first pair of models swished out through the curtains, the next group waiting in the wings. Knowing they weren't on for a while yet, Nina and Cat went to the nearby classroom that was serving as the girls' changing room. They entered through a mist of hairspray and perfume, and sidled past people preening in mirrors, checking their back views, searching for stray shoes, fluffing up their fringes. Every few moments, Preeyul ushered the next models across the corridor and up the steps that led to the stage. Nina marvelled at how clever Thea and Preeyul were with clothes and fabric – how inventive, adding the touches that turned an ordinary garment into something really eye-catching. A plain blue dress might have seemed ordinary if it hadn't been worn with a sash in bright, clashing fuchsia pink. Tweedy trousers looked cool and stylish worn with a high-necked lace blouse and Thea's trilby hat. A grey jacket had been transformed into something special with embroidered swirls of scarlet, worn with a tilted red beret. All the models had been given make-up and hairstyling that made them look as poised and polished as real catwalk models, though some of the boys had needed lots of persuading by Marissa to let her put make-up on them.

Nina wasn't used to it, either, and Marissa huffed at her as she tried to dab blusher on her cheeks. 'Don't scrunch up your face like that!'

'Cat, Nina – ready?' Preeyul called. 'Where's Linus?'

'Here!'

'OK. Wait for your cue ... and ... off you go!'

The entrance of Nina, Cat and Linus was the final one of the show's first half. Their music began; they erupted onto the stage, and Nina was so dazzled by the lights that there was no time to look for anyone in the audience or worry about the TV camera; no time for anything except to get to the end of the stage, pose, then turn and throw herself into a cartwheel, landing springily on her feet. They timed it so that Linus wheeled a beat later than Nina, Cat following – one, two, three. Nina lost her cap, ran back for it and improvised a hand-spring. There was a crash of applause, a few loud whoops, the lights rippled and flashed, and she found herself behind the curtain again, slightly dizzy, and wishing her part in the show wasn't over so quickly. The music faded, and people in the audience got to their feet, chatting and laughing.

'It's going brilliantly!' Thea said, backstage. 'Couldn't be better. Well done, everyone.'

For the show's finale, the Sixth Form boys and girls were dressed up as if for a leavers' ball, impossibly glamorous: the boys in waistcoats and bow ties, the girls in long dresses, with swept-up hair. Thea had choreographed a dance sequence for this section, finishing with each boy presenting his partner with a long-stemmed rose.

'Oh, don't they look *beautiful?*' Cat sighed. She and Nina had crept into the wings, ready for the curtain call.

Amidst all the excitement, laughter and even tears that followed the final applause and dimming of the lights, Nina thought what a great time she'd had. She felt proud. No one could say that the fashion show hadn't been a tremendous success, and she'd been part of it: a very small part, yes, but still a part. So had the aunts' shop, – this wouldn't have happened without Second-Hand Rose, so Aunts Rose and Nell could be proud of themselves too. So could Mr Fotheringay, for making the effort to come so soon after being ill, and Max, for coming to such a girly thing as a fashion show, and especially Jake, for coming even though he hated crowds.

*Every*one had been brilliant.

'I can't believe it's all over,' said Cat. 'Can't we do it again tomorrow night?'

21

The Green Crocodile

———◆◆◆———

The Eurostar terminal at St Pancras was huge, containing shops and people in an airy quietness. 'Like a cathedral,' Mum said.

Nina had never seen such a surprising building; the old-fashioned red brick that faced the Euston Road gave no hint of the soaring sleekness that opened up inside.

This was all so exciting, and new! Nina had never crossed the Channel before; she'd never left the country, and hadn't had a passport till two weeks ago. In just over an hour, she'd be on a train with Mum and Dad that would take them under the sea; by teatime they'd be in Paris. Paris! In Nina's mind, Paris was the impressionist paintings she'd seen in the art rooms at school – wide boulevards, and women with tiny waists and big hats; flowers, and rain, and pavement cafes, and circuses and dancers, and famous art galleries. She could practise speaking French to real French people!

'Fresh croissants,' Mum said, when Nina asked her what was the best thing about France. 'Supermarket ones just aren't the same. And French cafés. Fish soup, and cassoulet, and delicious dark chocolate mousse.'

'Hmm. Sounds like there'll be a lot of eating,' said Dad.

But, more importantly to Nina, there would be Alain and Adrien, the twins. Not brothers, not half-brothers, not even relations at all, but almost-brothers, she'd decided to call them. 'I'm going to Paris at half-term, to visit my almost-brothers,' had sounded very impressive indeed, when she'd told Max and Cat and Jake.

They collected their tickets from the machine; then Dad looked up at the big clock. 'We're in plenty of time. Shall we get a coffee, Mrs B, even if you'll say it's not as good as proper French coffee?'

He was only calling Mum 'Mrs B' to tease her. They'd been married now for two whole days, but Mum was keeping her own name. She couldn't imagine being called Mrs Bickerstaff, she said. It would seem like turning into someone else. But they were married, properly married; they both wore rings now, twisted gold rings that they'd exchanged at a ceremony called handfasting.

Neither Mum nor Dad had wanted a great frothy fuss of a wedding, so it had been a small but perfect occasion in the woods behind Tipton Hall, with just the aunts and Uncle Derek and a few good friends as guests, including Mr Fotheringay. Thea had made a gorgeous dress for Mum – upcycled, of course – dark, dark green and close-fitting, with leaf-shapes curling around the bodice. Perfectly, absolutely Mum. Nina's dress was plain green with a brilliant turquoise sash, and Dad had a leaf-patterned tie to wear with his dark-grey suit, so they all looked good together. Nina couldn't remember ever seeing Dad in a suit before, or Mum looking quite so beautiful.

She kept thinking about the day, going over and over it in her memory, like a special present she couldn't stop looking at, turning it in her hands to appreciate every detail. As Cat had said, it wasn't everyone who had the chance to go to their parents' wedding.

They sat with their coffees, and a milkshake for Nina, at a glass-fronted café, watching people in the main concourse coming and going with bags and wheeled cases and tickets. There were lots of children and families, as it was half-term.

Nina felt as if she wasn't really here. Half of her was already floating off to Paris: she was high inside the Eiffel Tower, or on a boat on the River Seine with her almost-brothers as tour guides, or in a café eating the delicious food Mum had talked about, served by real French waiters with lovely accents.

The other half of her was back at Second-Hand Rose. It seemed silly to be missing it, when she'd be away for just three nights, but she was.

It's Monday, she was thinking. Aunt Nell would be in charge, Aunt Rose either sorting out a muddle or making a new one. And it was Jake's afternoon at the shop, so he'd be on his way now, cycling down from Lumberforth on the brand new bike Mr Fotheringay had given him as a thank-you present. *Next* Monday, Nina would be back, helping Jake in the cellar after school, and catching up with the latest instalment of his life with llamas.

Thea might be there, changing the front window display. This was her regular weekly job now; the aunts had decided that it was well worth paying her to give it the special Thea touch. These days, the White Lady was looking extremely stylish, and the expression on her face seemed to show that she thoroughly approved of this new arrangement. Already sales had increased, because people stopped to look at the window and then drifted inside.

It might be one of the afternoons when Mr Fotheringay called in. Aunt Nell joked that the real purpose of his visits was to see Aunt Rose, which always made Aunt Rose go pink and pleased. But it was Aunt Nell who had suggested he came at least once a week, to check things over. Everyone had been amazed when the Chinese chess set sold at auction for nearly ten thousand pounds, and Aunt Nell didn't want to risk missing any other treasures.

The green crocodile would be somewhere in the shop, too. Nina smiled at the thought. After so many comings and goings, she'd convinced the aunts that the crocodile ought to stay, as a kind of mascot.

Its latest adventure had been to escape from the jaws of a dog – a lucky escape indeed. It had been rescued by Max; the crocodile's latest buyer had turned out to be Max's aunt, who'd thought her three-year-old son would like it. Simon had cuddled and played with it a few times before throwing it behind the sofa, where it stayed for at least two weeks, lost from view. No one noticed until Max and his parents went to visit, taking Zebedee, who soon sniffed it out. But Zebedee felt sure that the crocodile was too dangerous to be allowed in anyone's home. Dragging it from its hiding place, he savaged it with teeth and claws, ripping its stomach open and spilling stuffing all over the floor.

'Not like Zeb at all!' Max told Nina. 'He's usually such a soft old thing.'

Luckily, Simon had laughed uproariously at his crocodile's fate, rather than being upset. His mother was about to put the disembowelled toy in the dustbin when Max recognised it, and thought Nina would want to give it another chance. So his aunt put the mangled crocodile and its shed stuffing into a bag, and Max brought it back for Nina.

She wasn't the neatest person with a needle and thread, but she managed to shove the stuffing back inside and do a reasonable job of sewing up the torn felt, even if the stomach was a bit lumpy when she'd finished.

'Good as new!' Aunt Rose exclaimed, though only she could possibly think so.

At Nina's request, the crocodile now wore a red collar with a label saying NOT FOR SALE, and occupied various positions in the shop: sometimes by the till, sometimes sprawling on top of the books, and sometimes in the window, grinning nastily at passers-by.

The odd thing was that people kept wanting to buy it, now that they couldn't. 'Oh, not for sale? What a shame! You haven't got another one like it?'

'That's human nature for you,' said Aunt Nell. 'We certainly see a lot of that, here in the shop.'

'I know,' Aunt Rose agreed. 'And so much of it really is quite wonderful, isn't it, dear?'

Nina thought so, too.